LOVE'S GAMBLE

LOVE'S MAGIC SERIES BOOK 13

BETTY MCLAIN

This book is dedicated to anyone who has the courage to take a gamble on love.

CHAPTER 1

*L*anie was in a rush to get seven-year-old Christopher ready to catch the school bus. She sighed. It seemed like she was always in a rush. She never had a chance to do anything but rush around and try to keep herself and Chris in a place to live, with food, clothes, and other necessities. She was so tired of struggling to survive. Time was flying by, and she never had the chance to sit back and enjoy these years with her son.

He was growing up before her eyes, and all she could do was watch as he was shuffled from school to Sally's, and then home to bed. She had to work two jobs to make ends meet. Even on weekends, he had to stay with Sally, a grandmotherly neighbor of theirs, while Lanie worked.

Lanie didn't have a choice. She had no formal training. She had hooked up with Chris's dad straight out of high school. He shipped out the day after they married. He was only gone a week when she received word of his death because of sniper fire.

Two days after she received word of Ben's death, Lanie's dad died of a massive heart attack. Lanie's brother Bradley flew in from Arizona, where he lived with his wife and children, for the funeral.

After the funeral, he packed up their mom and carried her back to Arizona with him. Lanie was waiting for Ben's body to be shipped back for burial. She was also receiving a life insurance settlement. Ben had arranged it before he left. Ben's parents were waiting until after Ben's funeral, and then they were moving away. They had not approved of Ben and Lanie's marriage.

It was not until a month later Lanie began to suspect she was pregnant. She took a test, and it came back positive. The apartment did not allow children, so Lanie had to find another place to live. She put off moving at first. She had a hard time finding a place she could afford. The money from the life insurance would not last long. She knew she would have medical expenses when the baby was born. She finally found a small house where children were allowed. Having Sally for a neighbor was a plus. She helped Lanie every way she could. Having her there helped Lanie feel less alone.

Lanie found a job as a maid at a local motel, but it was only part-time work. She did not tell them she was pregnant at first. She knew she would be able to work for a while before she started showing. She wanted Ben's baby, but she was scared. Sally was her only backup support. When she told her mother about the baby, she thought she might get asked to move to Arizona, but no invitation was forthcoming.

Somehow Lanie made it through the months of her pregnancy. The lady in charge of the maids at the motel gave her a talking to for not telling them about the baby, but she didn't fire her.

When Chris was born, Lanie took one look and fell in love. Sally was there at the hospital with her. They both loved little Chris at first sight.

When Lanie had to go back to work, Sally would come over to Lanie's apartment and sit with Chris. Chris came to love her and called her Nana. Sally loved it. She had never had children, and Chris became her grandson in spirit.

As Chris got older, it got harder and harder to make ends meet. Sally would not accept any money from Lanie for keeping Chris. So,

Lanie made sure Sally had extra food whenever she went shopping. When Chris started kindergarten, he had to have a uniform and school supplies. So, Lanie started looking for work with better hours and better pay. She has no luck. The only thing she found was as a waitress at Stan's Bar and Grill. She took the job but kept the maid job also. Neither job paid enough for her to make it on one job alone. She only planned to be at Stan's until she found something else.

It was three years later, and she was still here, and there was no sign of an end in sight.

Lanie had been working for hours. Her shift was almost over, and she was more than ready to go home. Billy Joe and Bobby Joe Hall were sitting at a table with some friends drinking. Lanie knew both of them. They were twins and had been in school with her. They usually treated her okay. They flirted but did not get out of line. Tonight, they had been drinking for quite a while, and they were getting bolder.

Lanie saw two strangers come into the bar, and she was distracted for a minute. Billy Joe took advantage of her distraction to grab her and try to kiss her. She struggled to get away from him, but the alcohol had given him extra strength.

While she was struggling to get loose, she heard a voice behind her. "The lady asked to be turned loose," said the voice.

Billy Joe turned and looked at the stranger behind Lanie. He laughed. "This ain't no lady," he said. "This is just Lanie."

Lanie was furious. She drew back her cowboy boot-clad foot and kicked Billy Joe as hard as she could in the leg. "I may be just Lanie," she said. "But I am a lady, Billy Joe Hall, and don't you forget it."

Billy Joe howled and sat down, nursing his leg. Bobby Joe started to get up. Lanie gave him a hard look, and he sat back down. Lanie turned and nodded to the stranger. Then, she headed to the bar and a grinning George, the bartender.

"Thanks for all of your help, George," she said sarcastically.

"I knew you could handle them, Lanie. They don't mean any

3

harm. You know both Billy Joe and Bobby Joe have major crushes on you," said George.

Lanie made a scoffing sound. "I have told you all, repeatedly, I am not interested in either of the Hall brothers," said Lanie. "My shift is over. I'm heading home."

Lanie turned to leave. She saw the stranger and his friend having a drink at the bar. They had been listening to her conversation with George. The stranger who had tried to help her smiled at her. She smiled back and turned to leave.

Marcel Black Feather watched the waitress leave. Stanley White, his employee and friend, sat beside him. "Nice looking," said Stanley, watching Lanie leave the bar.

"Yeah," agreed Marcel. He and Stanley were on their way home after delivering a load of horses to the rodeo group in Harvey. They were about two hours from home when they decided to stop for gas and some food. After filling the tank, they spotted Stan's Bar and Grill. So, they went in for a burger and a drink.

When Marcel had seen the waitress being harassed, he had to step in. Women were not treated in such a way on the reservation. He grinned when he thought about the kick Lanie had delivered to her offender. The drunk got off lightly. He would not have wanted to tangle with Marcel.

Marcel and Stanley finished their food and drink and left to continue their journey. They had just started out of town when they saw a small, older model car pulled over to the side of the road with its hood up. The unmistakable figure of Lanie was standing by the car.

Marcel pulled to a stop behind Lanie's car, and he and Stanley got out and went forward. "Having trouble?" asked Marcel.

"Yes, it just quit. I managed to coast over to the side out of the road. I have no idea what the trouble is. I checked the gas. It has plenty."

Stanley had gone to look under the hood of the car. He turned back to Lanie. He had a broken cord in his hand. "This is your problem. The belt has broken. You have several more that are frayed and ready to break," said Stanley.

"Are they very expensive?" asked Lanie.

"They are different prices," said Stanley. "This one will probably be around seventy-five dollars. It will cost another fifty dollars to get it installed."

"Figures," said Lanie bitterly. "I only had one more payment on it."

"It looks like someone doctored it up to sell it. They hoped to get their money before the belts gave out," said Stanley.

"Can we give you a ride home?" asked Marcel.

Lanie looked at him and Stanley and the truck with the horse trailer behind it. Marcel saw her uncertainty.

"I'm Marcel Black Feather, and this is Stanley White. We are on our way back from delivering a load of horses. We live on the reservation just outside of Rolling Fork. It is about one hundred miles from here. We don't mean you any harm. We only want to help," said Marcel, holding out his hand for her to shake.

Lanie placed her hand in his. "Ouch," said Lanie, snatching her hand back from the shock of touching Marcel's hand.

"Sorry," said Marcel with a grin. "It must be static electricity."

"I guess," said Lanie, rubbing her hand.

Marcel was grinning because he knew he had met the woman meant for him. He turned slightly so Lanie would not see his grin. She might misunderstand.

"Will you let us give you a ride?" asked Marcel. Stanley was watching silently. He knew what the shock meant also.

"Okay," said Lanie. "I would appreciate a ride. It has been a long day, and I was not looking forward to walking home."

Stanley got into the backseat of the extended cab truck and left the front seat for Lanie. Marcel opened her door and helped her inside. The truck was large, and Lanie was wearing the short skirt that was part of her waitressing outfit. Marcel grinned as he enjoyed the amount of leg Lanie was showing. He went around the truck and got into the driver's seat. After he cranked the truck, he looked at Lanie.

She looked back at him, puzzled.

"Where do you live?" asked Marcel.

"Oh," said Lanie, flushing slightly. "I live in a housing project about two miles ahead."

Marcel pulled onto the road and went forward. He did not go too fast. He did not want to miss his turn.

Lanie guided them to a group of houses just off the road. There were about two dozen houses down a street. Half were on each side of the street. They all looked in bad repair. Marcel pulled his truck to a stop in front of the house Lanie pointed out as hers. He and Stanley got out and went with Lanie to the front door.

"You don't have to see me inside," said Lanie.

Marcel didn't answer. He had noticed the used bicycle and some other toys scattered around the yard.

"Are you married?" asked Marcel.

"No," said Lanie. "I'm a widow."

"I'm sorry," said Marcel. "You have children?"

"I have a seven-year-old son, Christopher," said Lanie with a smile.

Lanie had reached the door and opened it and started inside. She stopped abruptly. Sally was sitting in a chair watching Chris color a picture. She was fighting tears.

"What's wrong?" asked Lanie.

Sally looked at Lanie. She did not see Marcel and Stanley behind her.

"We all received notices today. They are going to tear down our houses and build condos," said Sally. "We have a week to find somewhere else to live. We are being evicted."

Lanie sank down in front of Sally on the floor. Sally looked up and spotted Marcel and Stanley. "I'm sorry. I didn't see you there," she said.

"Sally, this is Marcel Black Feather and Stanley White. They brought me home when my car quit on me," said Lanie.

"Oh no," said Sally. She looked at Marcel. "Thank you for helping Lanie."

"It was our pleasure," said Marcel, smiling at her.

Lanie was just sitting there, staring into space. She had no idea which way to turn. They could not afford to move. Without a car, she could not work. Lanie shook her head. "What are we going to do?" she whispered.

"You are coming home with me," said Marcel.

Lanie looked up, startled. "What?" she whispered.

"I need a housekeeper. I have a nice three-bedroom apartment. It is fully furnished. You all three could live there. We have a good school on the reservation, and there are lots of children for Christopher to play with."

"Why would you help us?" asked Lanie.

"People are supposed to help each other. The Great Spirit will not bless those who do not help when help is needed," said Marcel. Stanley turned away to hide a grin.

Lanie looked at Sally. "What do you think, Sally?"

"I think he is the answer to a prayer. I have been praying hard ever since I opened the letter," said Sally.

"Okay," said Marcel. "If you ladies will gather your personal belongings and anything else you want to keep, we have plenty of room in the horse trailer for them."

"You want us to move tonight?" asked Lanie.

"Why not. We are here. We have plenty of room, and you don't have much time," said Marcel.

"Why not indeed," said Sally, getting up. She looked at Stanley. "Young man, would you like to help me gather my things from the house next door?"

"It would be my pleasure, Ma'am," said Stanley following her out.

"Chris," said Lanie. "Go to your room and gather all of your toys and put them in a pillowcase. Then, put all of your clothes in another pillowcase. We are moving to a new place."

"Okay, Mom," said Chris. He looked at Marcel. Do you have horses?"

"Yes," said Marcel. "After we get you settled in and in school, I will teach you how to ride."

Chris had a big grin on his face as he hurried to his room to pack his things. Lanie went into her bedroom to start packing.

Marcel looked around. He went into the kitchen and looked through the cabinets. There was not a lot there. Marcel took the plastic bag of trash out of the trash can. He started taking down dishes and packing them in the can with towels and other cloths between them to keep them from breaking. When he had the can filled, he carried it and sat it by the front door. He found another can on the back porch and put the pots and pans in it.

He found a large ice chest and, dumping all of the ice in it, started packing the things in the refrigerator in it. He put it by the front door beside the other two containers.

There were a few pictures on the walls. Marcel took them down and laid them on the second-hand sofa. Lanie came back into the room with three pillowcases stuffed with her things. She looked surprised at first when she saw what Marcel had done. Then, she shrugged and put her things by the others at the door.

Marcel smiled at her, and she smiled back. "You don't realize how little you have until you start packing to leave," said Lanie.

"You are taking the most important things with you," said Marcel. "As long as you have Chris and Sally, nothing else matters. It can all be replaced."

Lanie smiled. "You are right. As long as I have my son and my friend, I am blessed."

"Here are my bags, Mom," said Chris, coming into the room.

"I'll take them," said Marcel. "I'm going to start taking some of these things and putting them in the trailer."

He picked up the can of dishes and went outside. Stanley was already out there, packing Sally's things into the trailer. They both left their loads and went back for more.

They soon had the trailer filled and were ready to go. Both ladies left their keys inside. After being told to leave, they did not think they owed anyone any consideration. They turned out all of the lights and closed the doors.

"What about my school?" asked Chris. "Don't I have to let them know I am leaving?"

"We can have the school on the reservation send for your records," said Marcel

"Okay," agreed Chris with a smile.

Sally climbed into the back seat, and Stanley took a seat beside her and showed her where the seat belt was. Chris got into the back seat between them, and Stanley fastened him in.

"Do you want to take the bicycle?" asked Marcel, pointing at the bike in the yard.

"No," said Chris. "It has a flat tire, and I am going to learn to ride horses now."

Everyone laughed, and with a considerably lightened atmosphere, they were prepared to start their journey to their new life.

$\mathcal{M}$arcel was about to start the truck when a car stopped in front of them.

Billy Joe and Bobby Joe got out of their car. Lanie sighed, and she and Marcel got out to speak with them.

"Are you all right, Lanie?" asked Billy Joe. "We saw your car on the side of the road, and we came to see if you were alright."

"I'm fine, Billy Joe. My car quit on me."

"Where are you headed?" asked Bobby Joe.

"They are going to tear down our houses and build condos," said Lanie. "We have been told to move."

"You know we will help you," said Billy Joe.

Lanie sighed. "I know you would, Billy Joe. I'm alright. I accepted a job as housekeeper from Mr. Black Feather. Sally is going with us, and we are moving to Rolling Fork."

"Black Feather," said Bobby Joe. "Are you with the family that furnishes racehorses?"

"Yes, I am," said Marcel with a nod.

"Oh. It's good to meet you," said Bobby Joe. "Your family raises some fine horses."

Marcel grinned. "Yes, we do," he agreed.

"I'm sorry," said Lanie. "Bobby Joe, Billy Joe, this is Marcel Black Feather. Marcel, this is Bobby Joe and Billy Joe Hall. They are not always drunken asses," Lanie ended with a smile.

"Aah, Lanie, I'm sorry about before. You know I didn't mean anything. I know you are a lady, and I would never treat you as less than one," said Billy Joe.

"I know, Billy Joe," said Lanie with a smile. "I'm not sorry I kicked you, though. You deserved it."

Billy Joe grinned sheepishly. "Yeah, I did," he agreed.

"It was nice to meet you," said Marcel. "But we need to get on the road. We have a long drive ahead of us."

Bobby Joe and Billy Joe each came forward and gave Lanie a hug. Lanie hugged them back and smiled at them. "You take care of yourself, Lanie, and if you need anything, just call us," said Bobby Joe.

"Thanks, guys. I will," promised Lanie.

Lanie turned toward the truck, and Marcel helped her into her seat again. Marcel nodded to Bobby Joe and Billy Joe and went to get in the driver's seat.

Bobby Joe and Billy Joe got in their car, and, with a wave to Lanie, they backed up and drove off.

Marcel cranked up and looked at Lanie. "Well, shall we try this one more time?" he asked.

They all laughed and started their trip in a much better mood.

Marcel drove around behind his house in just a little over two hours later. The journey had been pleasant. Stanley and Sally carried on a conversation, with a little help from Chris. Chris was very excited to be moving where there were horses. He had been fascinated with horses for some time but had not been able to spend any time around them.

Sally just enjoyed chatting with a new person. Her life had been very limited for quite some time. She loved taking care of Chris, but she was enjoying talking to an adult.

Stanley was enjoying the company, and he was looking forward to seeing Marcel and Lanie get to know each other. It should be quite an interesting time, he thought with a grin.

In the front seat, Lanie laid her head back and let the sound of voices lull her. She was excited but scared. She was ready to move forward. They had been stuck in this same cycle of struggle for the last seven years. Maybe, with Marcel's help, they could move forward. She sighed.

"Are you alright?" asked Marcel when he heard her sigh.

Lanie turned and smiled at him. "Yes, just tired. I feel like I have been moving at warp speed, and now I have to slow down. I guess I'm just scared."

Marcel nodded. "It's understandable. Don't worry, I won't let you fall, or if you do, I promise to catch you. You are not alone anymore."

Lanie felt tears well up in her eyes. She blinked to push them back. "Thank you," she said.

"For what?" he asked.

"For giving me hope," said Lanie.

Marcel reached over and squeezed her hand. He had to turn loose quickly because of the shock. "Well, it wasn't as bad this time," said Marcel.

Lanie laughed. "If we keep trying, in a few years, we may be able to touch without shocking each other," she said. Marcel looked at her and smiled.

Marcel stopped the truck and got out. He went around and helped Lanie out. Stanley was helping Sally and Chris out. Marcel led the way onto the back porch and unlocked the back door. They went through the kitchen where Lanie looked around, wide-eyed in amazement. Marcel went two doors down and opened a door. He stood back and let Lanie, Sally, and Chris enter. They stood looking around. Marcel came on in and moved over so Stanley could enter with some of their things.

"Where do you want me to put these, Boss?" asked Stanley.

Marcel went over and opened one of three doors. He then opened the other two.

"These are the bedrooms. Why don't we put Chris in the middle room? Sally can be on one side and Lanie on the other," said Marcel.

Lanie came out of her daze and went over and looked into Chris's room. She took the two pillowcases Stanley had into the room and laid them on the bed. She looked around. Chris was standing just inside the room, looking around. He had a very excited look on his face.

"Is this really going to be my room?" he asked.

Marcel came over and put an arm around Chris's shoulder. "Yes, Chris, this is your room. Do you like it?"

Chris looked at the stars on the ceiling. He looked at the planes and horses on the walls. He looked at the bed with the horses running on its spread, and he nodded. "I have never seen anything so great in my life," he whispered. "Yes, I like it."

Lanie felt her eyes tearing up again. She went over and hugged Chris. She looked up at Marcel and smiled. "Thank you," she said.

Marcel smiled back at her. "Let's let Chris unpack his things while I show you the rest of the apartment," he said.

Lanie went out with him after giving Chris another hug.

Sally had already claimed her room, and Stanley had been busy taking her things into it.

Marcel showed Lanie her room with an attached bath. She looked around but didn't linger. He showed her the living area they had already seen when they entered. Next was a small kitchen and a dining nook. There was also another bathroom.

Lanie shook her head. "Why do you have such a nice apartment in your house?" she asked.

"Well, I had a housekeeper living here. Her daughter is expecting a baby, and she is having a hard time of it. Little Fox and her son moved in with her daughter to take care of her and her family. She is not planning on returning, so I need someone to look after the place for me. I also have a small car you can use. I'll have Stanley park it by the back door for you. I will tell the stores on the reservation to let you get anything you need and add it to my account."

Marcel took out his wallet and peeled off five hundred-dollar bills. "This is your salary for two weeks. After we get you set up with a bank account, we can have your money deposited in it. If there is anything you need, just let me know. Tomorrow is Sunday, so you have another day before Chris has to register for school. I'll take you by the school and introduce you then."

"Do you know everyone?" asked Lanie, looking surprised.

"Just about," said Marcel. "I have lived here all of my life."

He smiled at Lanie. "It will be fine. You will fit right in. Before you know it, you will think of the reservation as home."

Lanie smiled. "I don't know whether to cry or pinch myself to make sure I'm not dreaming."

Marcel laughed. "You are not dreaming. I am very glad you are here. I am going to leave and let you get settled in. You don't have to start work until after we get Chris registered for school. There is plenty of food in the refrigerator. If anyone gets hungry, help yourselves. I'll show you all around the place after you get some rest. Good night."

"Good night, Marcel, thank you," said Lanie. Marcel just smiled and touched her shoulder as he left.

Stanley had finished bringing their things in, and Marcel met him in the kitchen. He gave him instructions to bring the small car around and leave the keys in it. "Sure thing, Boss," said Stanley with a smile as he went out.

Marcel did not notice the smile. He was too busy thinking about Lanie to pay any attention. He smiled to himself. "My true love is here," he whispered.

Marcel went into his office. He recorded the sale of the horses and added Lanie on as an employee. When he had his paperwork updated, he called Logan to let him know he and Stanley had returned.

"Hello, Marcel," said Logan.

"Hi. I just wanted to let you know we made it back okay," said Marcel.

"How did the sale go?" asked Logan.

"It went fine. They are going to want more horses next time. The next rodeo is an exhibition rodeo, and they are going to auction off some horses at the end and give the proceeds to the charity they are sponsoring. They want at least a dozen horses to auction off," said Marcel.

"We can manage a dozen more. We have extra since we are using the land we leased from May and Silas. Have you finished working on Dancing Eagle's old house?" asked Logan.

"It's almost done. I was thinking about seeing if Stanley would like to live there," said Marcel.

"We can ask him, but I think he likes being at the bunkhouse," said Logan.

"I should tell you, I have a new housekeeper. I brought her and her seven-year-old son back with me," said Marcel. "She is also my true love. She just doesn't know it yet," said Marcel.

"How do you know?" asked Logan.

"When we touched, we shocked each other. Besides, I felt it when we met," said Marcel. "I'm just giving her time to get used to me and the reservation," said Marcel.

"Congratulations and good luck," said Logan with a laugh. "Mom is going to be happy."

"Don't tell her yet. I don't want Lanie to find out from someone else before I get a chance to tell her. When you tell Willow, ask her not to tell," said Marcel.

"Okay, I'll tell Willow to not let anyone else know until you say it is okay," said Logan.

"I have to go. I want to have a quick look around before I get some rest. I'll talk to you tomorrow," said Marcel.

"Good night," said Logan.

Marcel hung up the phone and smiled. He should not have told about Lanie being his true love yet, but he could trust Logan, and he could not hold it inside any longer.

Marcel went out the back door and went to the barn. He turned on the light and walked around. They had three horses inside waiting to foal. He went by each one and petted and talked to them as he checked them out. They were all doing fine. Marcel looked around once more before turning the light off and leaving the barn.

Marcel made a circuit around the house and took a quick look at the garage and bunkhouse. He stood for a minute, looking up at the moon and stars when he reached the front porch.

He sighed. The sky looked beautiful tonight. He was glad to be home. He missed it when he had to make deliveries. He had Lanie now. Maybe he would let someone else do the deliveries from now on. Maybe Hank would like to make a few deliveries. Marcel grinned. Dawn would probably like to go along with him. She would leave her kids with Mom and jump at the chance of going away for a few days.

Marcel took one last look at the sky before going inside and locking up for the night.

Marcel checked the back door before going to his room. It was already locked. As he turned to go to his room, he saw Lanie in the door to the kitchen. She had taken a shower and was wearing pajamas and a robe; her feet were bare.

"Aren't your feet going to get cold?" asked Marcel with a grin.

"I'm used to going barefoot in the house," she said with a shrug. "This house is so warm, and the carpet is so soft; it is great."

Marcel laughed softly. "Did you need something?" he asked.

"I was going to see if I could find something to make a sandwich with," admitted Lanie, "It's been a while since I ate. I don't usually eat when I'm working."

Marcel went to the refrigerator and looked inside. "Well, let's see. There's some cold potato salad and some chicken salad." He took both out and set them on the counter. He opened a cabinet and brought out a loaf of bread.

"What would you like to drink?" asked Marcel.

"Do you have any milk?" asked Lanie.

"White or chocolate?" asked Marcel.

"Chocolate," said Lanie with a grin.

Marcel set the milk and chocolate syrup on the counter and reached into a cabinet for a glass. He handed Lanie a spoon and let her make her own chocolate milk.

Lanie stirred in the chocolate syrup and took a big swallow. She looked up with a grin. "It's good," she said.

Marcel laughed and handed her a napkin. "You have a mustache," he said.

Lanie took the napkin and wiped her face. "Did I get it?" she asked.

"Most of it," said Marcel. He took the napkin and wiped the remainder of the chocolate from her lips.

"Thanks," said Lanie as he gave her the napkin back.

"You're welcome," said Marcel.

"Do you want a chicken salad sandwich?" asked Marcel.

"Yes, please," said Lanie. "I can make it."

"I'm going to make me one too," said Marcel.

"Okay," said Lanie as she stood watching Marcel make two sandwiches.

"Do you want some potato salad?" asked Marcel.

"No, thank you. The sandwich will be plenty," she answered.

Marcel put the potato salad back in the refrigerator and took down two paper plates to put the sandwiches on. He took the plates to the table and pulled back a chair for Lanie to sit in.

Lanie sat in the chair and picked up her sandwich.

"Ummm, this is good," she said after eating a bite.

Marcel just smiled and bit into his sandwich.

"You shouldn't be waiting on me. I'm supposed to be waiting on you," said Lanie between bites.

"Not for a couple of days," replied Marcel. "You don't know your way around yet. I couldn't let us go to bed hungry," said Marcel. "I'm so glad you decided to come with us."

"I am too," said Lanie. "I think this is going to be a good move for all of us."

"So do I," agreed Marcel.

They finished their sandwiches, and Marcel took their plates and threw them away. Lanie brought their glasses into the kitchen. Marcel rinsed them out and left them in the sink.

"Thanks for the sandwich. I'll say good night now," said Lanie.

"Good night, Lanie. I'll see you in the morning," said Marcel.

CHAPTER 3

*L*ogan and Willow came by first thing the next day. When Logan told her Marcel had found his true love, Willow could not wait to meet her. They had Joey and Camille with them. Marcel was standing by the corral fence, watching some horses. Lanie and Chris were with him. They had finished breakfast, and Chris could not wait to see some horses. He was standing beside Marcel, wide-eyed with excitement. Lanie was smiling at him indulgently.

They all looked around when Logan's car stopped near them. Logan opened the car door and let Joey out first. While Logan was helping Willow out with Camille, Joey ran over to Marcel.

"Hey, Uncle Marcel," he said as he gave him a hug. Marcel hugged him back and, picking him up, twirled him around. Joey squealed delightedly. He loved being swung around.

When Marcel put him on his feet, he looked at Chris and grinned. "Hi," said Joey.

Chris grinned back. "Hi," he said.

"Joey," said Marcel. "This is Christopher. He likes to be called Chris. Chris, this is my nephew Joey."

"Hi, Chris," said Joey.

"Hi, Joey," said Chris.

"Uncle Marcel, can we play in the treehouse?" asked Joey.

"If it's okay with your moms," said Marcel.

"What treehouse?" asked Lanie.

"It's safe," said Willow, who had joined them. "It's in a large tree between the house and the barn. The children play in it all of the time."

"Please, Mom," begged Chris.

"Okay, but you be careful," said Lanie.

"Joey, watch out for Chris. He has not been in the treehouse before," said Willow. The boys ran off to play in the treehouse. Willow turned to Lanie and smiled. "Hi, I'm Willow, Logan's wife," she said.

"I'm sorry," said Marcel. "Willow, this is Lanie Melton. She's my new housekeeper. Lanie, as she already told you, this is Willow, Logan's wife. This big lug here beside me is my brother, Logan."

"It's nice to meet you, Lanie," said Logan. "I hope you like it here on the reservation."

"I haven't seen much of the reservation. But what I have seen I love," said Lanie. She turned to Willow. "What a beautiful baby," she said. Camille smiled up at her with a wide toothless smile. Lanie couldn't help but smile back. Camille reached her arms out to Lanie. "May I hold her?" asked Lanie.

"Sure," said Willow, handing her over. Lanie took Camille in her arms and then sat her on her hip. It felt so natural to be holding a baby again. Chris had grown so fast. Lanie felt like the holding time was gone before she was done enjoying it.

Marcel smiled, and Willow and Logan exchanged a pleased look. They were happy with Marcel's lady. Marcel did not notice their look. He was focused on Lanie. "Would you like to come inside and maybe have a glass of tea?" Lanie asked Willow and Logan.

"Maybe next time," said Logan. "We are on our way to Mom and Dad's. Mom is preparing Sunday dinner. She would have called you if she knew you were back. Why don't you bring Lanie and Chris over and introduce them?" asked Logan.

"I don't want to intrude," said Lanie.

"It wouldn't be an intrusion. Mom loves company, and she especially loves to keep up with everything going on in her boys' lives," said Logan.

Lanie looked at Marcel uncertainly. "He is right; Mom would love to have you and Sally and Chris join us for dinner," said Marcel.

"Who's Sally?" asked Logan.

"That would be me," said Sally coming out to join them.

"Logan, Willow, this is Sally Stow. She is Chris's honorary grandmother. Sally, this is Marcel's brother, Logan and his wife, Willow, and this is Camille," said Lanie.

"It's nice to meet you all," said Sally.

"It's nice to meet you," said Logan coming forward and shaking her hand. Willow smiled and agreed.

"Hello, Camille," said Sally smiling at the baby. Camille reached out her arms for Sally. Lanie laughed and let her go to Sally. Sally started talking baby talk to her. Camille laughed and gurgled words back at her. Everyone laughed at Camille's attempt at communication.

"Camille loves going to Mom's house," said Willow. "She has everyone there wrapped around her small fingers."

"Joey," called Logan. "We have to go." Joey and Chris came running.

"The treehouse is great," said Chris to Lanie. Lanie put an arm around him and gave him a squeeze. She was so pleased to see her son so happy.

"Are you coming to Mom's dinner?" asked Logan as he helped his family into the car.

Marcel shrugged. "Sure. If it's alright with Lanie and Sally, we will come."

Lanie looked at Sally. Sally nodded. She wanted Lanie and Chris to be happy here. She was sure Lanie and Marcel had a future together. She was going to do all in her power to encourage them to be with each other.

"We will be on in a little while," said Marcel as he waved Logan and Willow off.

After Logan was gone, they all went inside, cleaned up, and changed clothes to go to the Black Feather family home for dinner. Lanie was still a little apprehensive. She was afraid they would be intruding. She shrugged her shoulders. Marcel said no. She would just have to trust he would know. After all, they were his family.

Marcel called Stanley and asked him to bring his car to the front of the house. Marcel invited Stanley to go along, but he declined. He had a date in town.

When they came out of the front door, Marcel's SUV was sitting waiting for them with a booster seat already installed for Chris. They piled into the car with Sally seated beside Chris. Marcel reached over and squeezed Lanie's hand. "Only a small shock this time," he said with a smile.

"It's hardly noticeable," answered Lanie with a smile.

They arrived at the Black Feather family home to find children running around playing and the men sitting on the porch watching them while the ladies were inside helping Daisy fix dinner.

Joey ran over as soon as they stopped to get Chris to play with them. Chris looked at Lanie for permission, and she nodded. Chris wasted no time joining his new friend.

Marcel took Sally's and Lanie's arms and guided them to the porch.

"Sally, Lanie, this is part of my family," he pointed at Glen. "This is my dad, Glen; my brothers, Leon, Mark, and Logan. And my sister's husband, Hank. Gentlemen, meet Sally Stow and Lanie Melton. Lanie is my new housekeeper."

"We're glad you are here, ladies," said Glen. There was a round of "nice to meet you" from the rest of the guys except Logan, who smiled and nodded.

"It's nice to meet you all," said Lanie and Sally.

"I'm going to take Lanie and Sally inside to meet Mom," said Marcel. "I'll be back in a minute. I want to talk to you about something, Dad.

Glen nodded as Marcel opened the front door and guided the ladies inside. He headed for the kitchen where he could hear voices. The voices stopped when Marcel entered with Sally and Lanie. Willow smiled at the ladies, and Daisy hurried over, with Camille in her arms, to hug Marcel and look curiously at his guests.

"I'm glad you made it back home safely," she said.

"Mom, this is Sally and Lanie. Lanie is my new housekeeper," said Marcel.

"Welcome, Lanie and Sally. We are glad you joined us. These are my daughters-in-law, Doris, Glenda, and Willow, and my daughter Dawn," said Daisy.

"We've met," said Willow. They all smiled and welcomed the ladies into the group.

"You've met?" questioned Doris.

"Yes, Logan and I stopped by Marcel's on the way over to make sure he knew about Sunday dinner, and he introduced us to Lanie and Sally," answered Willow.

"I need to talk to Dad. Is dinner going to be long?" asked Marcel.

"You have about thirty minutes," said Daisy.

"Okay," said Marcel. He squeezed Lanie's hand before he left to go back outside.

All the ladies noticed Lanie's jump when Marcel squeezed her hand and how she was rubbing it afterwards. They looked at each other and smiled. No one said anything. They were going to let the couple discover their connection for themselves. They all gathered around and included Lanie and Sally in the dinner preparations and made them feel welcome.

Marcel went back outside to the porch. He sat down in a chair close to Glen. Glen waited patiently for Marcel to speak. "The housing project where Lanie and Sally were living is being torn down to build condos. They received letters yesterday giving them one week to move or be evicted. They were blindsided. They had no idea this was in the works. Lanie and Sally are okay, but there are almost two dozen other families who are stranded with nowhere to go. I was wondering if you could talk to Angelica and see if the Black Foundation could look into it and maybe help those families somehow." Marcel paused and looked at his Dad.

"Yeah, my friend Nick and his family are still there," said Chris, who had come up behind Marcel and had been listening.

Marcel turned and put his arm around Chris and drew him to his side. "Does Nick have a mother and dad?" asked Marcel.

Chris nodded. "A sister too; they did live on a farm but had to move. Nick's dad has been working driving a delivery truck."

"What is Nick's last name?" asked Glen.

"Stavos," said Chris.

Glen pulled a pad from his pocket and wrote Nick Stavos on it. "Where is this town?" asked Glen.

"It's a little town about one hundred miles southwest of here called Liberty," said Marcel.

"Do you have the address of the houses to be torn down?" asked Glen.

Marcel took a slip of paper from his pocket and handed it to Glen. "I wrote down Lanie's address," said Marcel.

Glen took the address and his tablet and went inside. Everyone followed him inside and took seats to wait and see what would happen. Glen went over to a table and picked up his phone. He pulled out the chair by the table and sat down. He laid his tablet and pen and the piece of paper in front of him and dialed Angelica Steel.

"Hello, Alex, this is Glen Black Feather. I was wondering if I could talk to Angelica," said Glen.

"Sure, I'll get her," said Alex as he laid the phone down and went to call Angelica to the phone.

Angelica came into the room and handed Alex their daughter to hold while she came to answer the phone. Alex took his daughter and sat down on the floor and started playing with her. Angelica smiled and went to answer the phone.

"Hello, Glen, what can I do for you?" asked Angelica.

"Sorry to bother you on Sunday, Angelica, but this situation is rather urgent," said Glen.

"It's fine, now tell me what's wrong."

"My son, Marcel, just came back from delivering some horses. He came through a small town called Liberty; it is about one hundred miles southwest of here. They have a small housing project with about two dozen houses in it. All of the residents received notices yesterday that the houses are being torn down to build condos. These are poor people with very little income, and they were given one week to get out or be thrown out. Marcel helped two of the residents, but I was wondering if the Black Foundation could look into the situation and see if they could help."

Angelica had been making notes as Glen talked. "Do you have the address of the housing project?" she asked. Glen read off the address Marcel had given him. "I will get the foundation on it," said Angelica.

"Thanks, Angelica," said Glen. "There is one more thing. There is a family there called Stavos. It's a man, his wife, and two children. If he is agreeable to working for our family, we will find a place for him and his family. We will go and move him if he is okay with it. Just let us know."

"Thank you for bringing it to my attention. I'll let you know about the Stavos family," said Angelica. Angelica hung up and called the director of the Black Foundation and told him to check it out today and get back to her.

Glen hung up the phone and found he had a large audience. Lanie and Sally had tears on their faces, and Daisy came over and kissed Glen.

"Thank you," said Lanie. Marcel went to her and drew her into his arms.

Chris came over too. "Mr. Black Feather asked them to bring Nick and his family here," said Chris.

"Lanie pulled back from Marcel and smiled at her son. "I know. I heard him," she said. Chris turned and ran outside to tell his new friend that his old friend may be joining them.

"Tell everyone dinner is ready. And have the children wash their hands," said Daisy. She kissed Glen one more time before heading back into the kitchen with all of the ladies following.

They had one table for children and one for adults. The children's plates were all fixed with drinks at each plate. The adult table had plates and silverware, but the food was in the middle of the table, waiting to be passed around. The iced tea was on the counter, along with glasses waiting for each person to get their own.

Chris came in with the other children and happily sat beside Joey at the children's table. All of the children came in and sat down, but they did not start eating. They were waiting for the adults and the blessing.

When everyone was seated, they all joined hands and bowed their heads. Glen asked the blessing and added a bit at the end thanking the Great Spirit for bringing Lanie, Chris, and Sally into their family. Lanie flushed slightly and sent first Glen, then Marcel, a smile. They both smiled back at her. Marcel squeezed her hand. He was sitting next to her.

They all enjoyed the meal and the talk. To Lanie, it seemed as if there was a lot of talk. She sat, quietly listening. She looked around and watched everyone talking and enjoying each other's company. Even Chris, at the children's table, was talking to everyone as if he had known them all of his life. She sighed. It was all just too good to be true.

"What's wrong?" asked Marcel softly.

"Nothing is wrong. Everything is wonderful. I can't believe I'm not dreaming. I keep thinking I'm going to wake up in the tumble-down house in Liberty," Lanie replied quietly.

"You are not dreaming. You are very much awake, and you are

never going back to the tumbledown house in Liberty," said Marcel quietly but forcefully. He squeezed her hand, and they both felt the shock. It was not as bad as before.

"I guess we are getting in sync with each other," grinned Marcel. Lanie smiled at him.

Everyone at the table had been watching Marcel and Lanie, but they made sure the two were not aware of their attention.

CHAPTER 4

When they had finished dinner and cleaned the kitchen, they all went outside to sit and talk—all except Glenda and Willow, who were putting their babies down for a nap. Marcel managed to snag one of the swings and had seated Lanie beside him. No one objected. They were all for promoting true love.

"How is the work coming on Dancing Eagle's house?" Marcel asked Logan.

"It's almost finished," said Logan. "Laughing Elk and his crew put a new roof on. They had the electric company run wires to the house and light fixtures inside. They added a bathroom and piped water inside from the pump. They painted it inside and out. It is small, but it has two bedrooms, a living room, and a kitchen. There is also a loft. It could be used as another bedroom."

"It didn't have a bathroom?" asked Marcel.

Logan laughed. "No. Dancing Eagle used an outdoor toilet. I also had Laughing Elk get rid of the outhouse and fill it in."

"Good," said Marcel. "We wouldn't want anyone falling in it."

Some of the guys laughed.

"No, we wouldn't want that," agreed Glen. "Are you thinking about putting the Stavos family in Dancing Eagles house?"

"If he has lived on a farm, he should be familiar with horses. All he would have to do would be ride fences and repair any broken ones and watch out for rustlers," said Marcel. "I thought we could ask him about it."

"It's a good idea. We can ask him. We would have to arrange for his children to have a ride to school."

"We will work it out if they come," said Glen.

They were sitting there quietly talking to each other when Glen's phone rang. He reached into his front shirt pocket and answered. He had been keeping it in his pocket since he had talked to Angelica.

"Hello, Glen, this is Angelica. My director at the foundation just reported to me. They have talked to all of the residents in the housing to be demolished in Liberty. Four of the families had already made arrangements to move in with relatives. We will check back with them later to be sure they are alright. The Stavos family is being brought to you. They were very happy to have somewhere to go. The foundation has placed six of the families, and they are working on finding places for the remaining seven families. Where do you want the Stavos family delivered?"

"Bring them to Marcel's house. He can get them situated. Thank you, Angelica. I appreciate such fast work," said Glen.

"I like pushing my weight around," said Angelica with a laugh. "I'll keep you updated on the others."

They hung up, and Glen turned to his interested audience.

"The Stavos family is being brought here. They are going to bring them to you, Marcel, so you will have to decide where to put them," said Glen. Marcel nodded and waited for the rest. "Four of the families have moved in with relatives, and the Black foundation found homes for six families. They are working on finding places for the remaining seven families. Angelica will let me know what happens," said Glen.

Lanie shook her head. "You people are the nicest people I have ever met. My own brother would not offer me a home when I was alone and pregnant. Here you step right in and help all of these families find places to live. If there was such a thing, I would nominate you all for an angel award. That is what you all are, angels," said Lanie. She smiled mistily and squeezed Marcel's hand. She hardly even noticed the shock. It felt so good feeling her hand in his.

"We are not angels. We are just people trying to do the best we can," said Marcel.

"Speak for yourself," said Logan. "If she wants to think I'm an angel, it is fine with me."

Willow hit his arm. "You are no angel, Logan Black Feather," she said. Everyone laughed as Logan kissed Willow.

"Where is Camille?" asked Logan.

"She is sleeping. I slipped out," said Willow.

"Marcel," said Daisy. If you need furniture for Dancing Eagle's house, we have some stored in the garage. We put it out there when I redecorated. I'm sure you will be able to find anything you need in there. We can call Billy Fox and have him install a stove and refrigerator. Do you want me to call him?" asked Daisy.

"Thanks, Mom," said Marcel. "How about you guys help me look over the furniture in the garage and find what is needed. You can come and look, too." Marcel said to Lanie. The guys all went with Marcel to look over the furniture. He held onto Lanie's hand and took her along with him.

Lanie gasped when Marcel opened the garage door, and she saw the furniture stored there. "This is great," she said. "Anyone would love having any of this furniture."

Logan and Mark picked a sofa and carried it outside. Leon and Hank each carried out a rocking chair. Logan and Mark came back and picked out a table and four chairs. They carried out the table, and Marcel and Lanie took two chairs each.

They all went back in and started looking at bedroom sets. They found a double bed and dresser and took them out. They carried out a mattress and box springs set for the bed. There was a bedside table;

it was taken to join the other furniture outside. They found two twin beds with mattresses and springs and decided they would do for the children since the rooms were small. They added a small dresser and a small chest. "We can always come back and get more if we need to," said Logan.

"Yes," agreed Marcel. "We need to take this furniture and see how well it fits in the house. Let's ask Dad if we can use his trailer and take the furniture on over." They all headed for the porch to ask about the trailer.

Glen gave permission for the use of the trailer, and Daisy came out and told them Billy Fox was having two of his men deliver and install a stove and refrigerator. The guys went to load up the furniture, and Lanie sat on the porch with the women.

Daisy went inside and looked through her linen closet. She found a double set of sheets and two twin sets. She added some bath towels and some small towels for the kitchen. She came out on the porch and gave them to Lanie. She had put them all in a pillowcase to make them easier to carry.

"Will you take these to Marcel so he can take them with him?" she asked.

"Sure," said Lanie with a smile. She took the pillowcase and headed to the garage, where the guys were almost done loading furniture.

"Your mom sent these for you to take with you," said Lanie.

"Thanks," said Marcel with a smile as he took the pillowcase.

"We are about ready to take the furniture over to the house. Do you want to wait here until I get back?" asked Marcel.

"Well, I could take your SUV, and you could have your brothers drop you at home on the way back. We don't know when the Stavos family is going to arrive. I would hate for them to get there and find no one at home," said Lanie.

"Stanley and Milo will be there. They would have them wait for us," said Marcel. "I don't mind you taking my SUV if you are ready to go home."

"I think I will," said Lanie. "I am tired. It's been a busy couple of days."

"Okay, let's round up Chris and Sally and get you started for home. I'll see you there as soon as we get the furniture unloaded," said Marcel. They called Chris and headed for the porch to collect Sally and tell everyone goodbye.

"I want to thank you for having us as part of your family dinner," Lanie said to Daisy.

"We are delighted you came. If you ever need anything, you just call. You are part of our family now," said Daisy. "Sally, you make sure Milo brings you to bingo with him next Thursday night."

"I surely will," agreed Sally. "Thanks for telling me about it. I'm looking forward to seeing the community center."

"It still has some decorations from Silas and May's wedding. They had a double wedding with his brother, Jamie, and May's sister, April, but it was decorated for May and Silas, so everyone refers to it as May and Silas's wedding decorations," said Daisy with a laugh.

"We'll see you later," said Lanie.

Chris was waving goodbye to all of his new friends. He had a very happy look on his face. This move had been great for him, thought Lanie.

She carefully drove away from the house and out to the road, keeping a careful lookout for children. It was a short trip, and they were soon pulling up in front of Marcel's house and parking there.

Stanley saw them come back and came over to see where Marcel was. Lanie explained about the guys taking the furniture to Dancing Eagle's house for the Stavos family.

"They are on their way here?" asked Stanley.

"Yes," agreed Lanie.

"I wonder if the boss has thought about getting them some food," said Stanley.

"I don't know. He didn't say anything about it," said Lanie.

"Well, I can always run to the store after he gets back," said Stanley. He headed back to the bunkhouse, and Lanie followed Sally and Chris inside.

They went to their apartment, where Sally went to turn on the television. Chris followed her to see what was on. They both settled down to watch television and relax. Both of them looked very contented. Lanie went back to the main room of the house. She wanted to be close to the door in case she was needed.

She walked around the room, looking at all of Marcel's pictures. They were mostly of his family. Some were pictures of horses. It was not surprising to see horses since he was in the business of raising horses. It looked like he was especially fond of a couple of them. Lanie smiled. You couldn't blame him, she thought. They were very nice-looking horses.

Lanie was curious about the rest of the house, but she knew Marcel wanted to show her around, so she decided to wait for him. She didn't want to disappoint him after he had done so much for them and their friends.

She heard a car stop out front and went to look. It was Marcel. Logan and Mark were dropping him off. He waved goodbye and came inside. Marcel smiled at Lanie. "It sure is nice to see a pretty face when I get home," said Marcel with a smile at Lanie.

Lanie smiled. "Stanley was here when we came in. He was wondering if you had provided any food for the Stavos family. I told him I didn't know. I think he was going to check with you when you arrived. I think he is here," said Lanie as a knock sounded on the door.

Marcel went to open the door. "Mom had Billy Fox deliver food along with a refrigerator," said Marcel.

Stanley laughed. "Your mom has a way of getting things done," said Stanley.

"Yes, she does," Marcel laughingly agreed.

"I'll see you later, Boss," said Stanley as he left.

Marcel closed the door and turned to Lanie and smiled.

"Now, all we have to do is wait for the Stavos family to get here," remarked Marcel.

"Are you hungry? I could fix you something to eat," said Lanie.

"No, I'm still full from Mom's dinner," said Marcel. "Why don't we sit and talk while we wait?" asked Marcel. "We can get to know each other better."

"Sure," said Lanie, taking a seat on the sofa beside Marcel.

Marcel reached over and took her hand. There was only a small shock this time, so he kept a hold of her hand.

Lanie looked at their hands. She didn't object. She liked the feel of her hand in his. It gave her a warm, safe feeling.

"I wanted to see if we still got a shock," explained Marcel, looking at their hands.

Lanie smiled. "It's not as bad as it was at first. Now it's more like a welcoming twinge."

Marcel laughed. "Welcome to my home and my life, Lanie," he said.

"Thank you," said Lanie with a smile. "For making me so welcome in your home and your life," said Lanie.

Marcel squeezed her hand. He let go and went to answer the door. The Stavos family had arrived. Lanie went with him to the door.

When they opened the door, Randell and Merry looked a little apprehensive, but when they saw Lanie, they relaxed some and smiled.

"Hello, Merry. Hello, Randell. Where are Joy and Nick?" asked Lanie.

"They are outside," said Merry. "They waited with the people from the Black Foundation while Randell and I came to see where we were going."

"Come in," said Marcel, holding the door open and inviting them in.

"My family raises horses. We sell them to the racing foundation. We have a place leased next to our place. It has a small house on it.

The house has been refurbished and has some furniture in it. Chris said you had worked on a farm. I thought you and your family could live there and you could keep an eye on the horses. You would have to ride fences and repair them and keep an eye out for rustlers. Do you think you would like to try it out?" asked Marcel.

"Yes," said Randell, nodding vigorously.

Marcel held out his hand. "I'm Marcel Black Feather. I can take you to the house now so you can get settled in before dark. There may be problems. The house has just been worked on, but we can fix any problems if you bring them to my attention."

Randell shook his hand, and Merry smiled. "Thank you, Mr. Black Feather. I promise you won't regret helping us."

"Let's get you home," said Marcel.

"Don't leave yet," said Lanie. "I need to get Chris so he can say 'hi' to Nick."

"Okay, we'll be outside," said Marcel as he turned to show Randell and Merry out.

Lanie hurried to tell Chris and Sally the Stavos family had arrived. "Chris, Nick and his family are outside. I thought you might want to say 'hi' before Marcel takes them to their new house," said Lanie.

"Oh, yeah," said Chris, jumping up excitedly and heading for the front door. Sally followed along with Lanie as they followed Chris.

They found Chris, Nick, and Joy all smiles, talking excitedly. Marcel was talking to the people from the Black Foundation and making arrangements for them to follow him over to the Stavos' new house. Sally greeted Merry and Randell and told them they would not be sorry they took the chance for a better life.

"The Black Feather family is a very good family. You could not have ended in better hands," said Sally. "You can trust them all, but especially Marcel. He's a really good guy."

Marcel heard her and grinned. He came over and hugged Sally. "Thank you, Sally. I'm glad you decided to join my family," said Marcel.

Sally flushed slightly but accepted the hug and smiled at Marcel. "I'm glad, too," she said.

Lanie had been watching them with a smile. Marcel turned to her. "I'm going to show the way and help them get settled. I'll be back later," he said as he squeezed her hand.

Lanie nodded and smiled. She drew Chris back away from the car as Marcel got in his SUV. Stanley joined him to go along in case he was needed at the house. Lanie, Chris, and Sally all waved as the cars pulled away.

When the cars were gone, Lanie and Sally led Chris back inside. She offered to fix them something to eat, but they both said they were not hungry. They went back to watching the show Lanie had interrupted with the news of the Stavos family's arrival.

CHAPTER 5

*L*anie sat down and watched television with them, but her mind was not on the show they were watching. She thought about the last two days. Things had changed fast for them. She had been at the end of her rope when Marcel tossed her another rope and pulled her out of the mess her life had become. She went from having no hope to thinking they had a chance at a future. She knew there was an attraction between her and Marcel. She didn't know if it was real or if she was just feeling this way because Marcel had rescued them. She had to be sure her feelings were real or just feelings of gratitude for him saving her and Chris.

It had been a long time since Ben died. They had been so young. They had not known what love was. If he had lived, they might have grown into their feelings. They never had the chance to find out. She was left with her son, whom she loved dearly, and finding a way to survive for both of them.

Lanie sighed. Yes, she was attracted to Marcel, but she was not ready to act on the attraction. She was going to take her time and let him get to know them and let them get to know him. There was no rush. This was their lives, and she wanted to be sure she made the right decisions for herself and her son.

Sally turned off the television and told Chris it was bedtime. Chris didn't argue but went to get ready for bed. Lanie turned to Sally.

"I should have been paying attention. You should not have to tell Chris to go to bed," said Lanie.

Sally shrugged with a smile. "You have a lot on your mind. Besides, he is used to me telling him what to do. It is easy now. Just wait a couple of years, and I suspect we will have a harder time getting him to listen. Enjoy the peace while you can," Sally finished with a laugh.

"You are probably right," agreed Lanie.

"I am headed to bed," said Sally. "You can make sure Chris is in bed."

"Okay," agreed Lanie.

Lanie straightened the room and then went to check on Chris. He was in bed but not asleep. "Good night," said Lanie, leaning over to give him a kiss on top of his head."

"Good night," said Chris. "I am so glad we moved here."

"So am I," answered Lanie. "Sleep now; I'll see you in the morning. We have to get you registered in school."

"School will be great," said Chris. "Joey and Nick will be there."

Lanie smiled. "Yes, sleep now." Lanie turned out the light but left the door cracked, so there was some light in the room. She waited on the sofa, trying to read a book she had started. She finally put the book down. She could not concentrate on the plot. Her mind had too many things going around in it. She decided to fix Marcel a light meal for when he returned. He should be hungry after helping the Stavos family get settled.

Lanie looked in the refrigerator and smiled. Marcel must like chicken sandwiches. There was a stack of containers of chicken salad. He might like what came out of the container, thought Lanie, but wait until he got a taste of her fresh chicken salad. She couldn't make it tonight. There was no fresh chicken, but soon, she would surprise him.

Lanie took out some ham, eggs, and cheese and laid them on the counter. She added some diced onion and diced pepper. She found a pan and put butter in it to melt. After mixing eggs and cheese and diced ham, she put in the diced onion and pepper. She added salt and pepper and mixed it well. Lanie checked the pan and, satisfied the pan was warm and the butter melted, she poured the mixture into the pan. While it was cooking, she put bread in the toaster. When the omelet was ready, she flipped it over and folded it in half. The toast popped up, and she put in two more slices. While the toast was cooking, Lanie took two plates from the cabinet and halved the omelet. She put half on each plate. The toast popped up, and she put two slices on each plate.

Lanie found some tea in the refrigerator and filled two glasses with ice. She set them on the counter to wait for Marcel before pouring the tea. She heard the front door close and turned to fill the two glasses with tea.

"What smells so good?" asked Marcel as he entered the kitchen.

"I thought you might be hungry," said Lanie smiling.

"If I wasn't before, I am after smelling this great aroma," said Marcel, taking his glass of tea from her and pulling her chair back for her to sit.

Lanie smiled and sat in the chair. Marcel took his chair and breathed in deep. "It smells almost too good to eat," said Marcel.

"It's just an omelet," said Lanie. "It's fast and easy to make."

"You'll have to show me how to make it," said Marcel.

"Why would I teach you how to make it? It is my job to make it," said Lanie.

"It's not your job to work all hours," said Marcel, taking her hand and ignoring the shock. "I don't expect you to work around the clock. "We will have to decide which hours suit you best and set up a schedule."

"I'm not worried about any of that," said Lanie. "I've hardly done anything since I have been here."

Marcel shrugged. "You are still getting settled in. Some days there will not be much to do, but other days we may be very busy. Anytime you need time off, you tell me, and I'll make sure someone handles things. I am not a slave driver."

Lanie laughed. "Anyone less like a slave driver would be hard to find," she said.

They finished their food, and Marcel helped her clean up, over her objections. They said their goodnights with Marcel giving her hand another squeeze and smiling as he gazed into her eyes. He tore his eyes away and turned away. Lanie opened the door to her room and went inside without looking back to see Marcel gazing after her with longing.

Lanie made breakfast the next morning and packed Chris a lunch. She went to his door and opened it to remind him to come and eat. Sally stuck her head out of her door and sniffed. "I smell coffee," said Sally.

Lanie laughed. "It's made, and breakfast is on the table."

Sally hurried over to the coffee maker to fill a cup with coffee. She took a big drink and went to the table where she took her seat and smiled at Chris.

Marcel came in the back door. He had been out in the barn, checking on the horses that were about to foal. He reminded Stanley and Milo to keep an eye on them while he was taking Lanie to register Chris in school. "I thought we could go by and pick up the Stavos family and let them get registered, too," said Marcel.

"Does the bus run where they are?" asked Lanie.

"I don't know," said Marcel. "I'll have to find out."

"Sit down and eat," said Lanie, pouring him a cup of coffee. "Do you want cream or sugar?"

"Black is fine," said Marcel as he accepted the cup and sat at the table.

Lanie came over to take her seat, and Marcel stood to hold her chair. Lanie smiled at him and sat down to eat. Everyone dug in. The food disappeared quickly, and Sally shooed them out of the kitchen.

"You all get going," she said. "I can put a few dishes in the dishwasher."

"Thanks, Sally," said Lanie as she handed Chris his lunch and started him toward the front door.

When they stopped in front of the Stavos home, Randell came out. Marcel explained about taking the children to register for school, and Randell went back inside to tell Merry, Joy, and Nick.

They were all back out in just a few minutes. Joy and Nick joined Chris on the back seat, and Randell and Merry sat in the two middle seats. After checking to be sure everyone was buckled in, Marcel headed for the school.

When they parked in front of the school and went in, they met the principal in the hall. He was keeping an eye on the children before class. He smiled when he saw Marcel come in with a crowd.

"Good morning, Marcel, I see you have found us some new students," said Principal Leopard.

"Yes, they have just moved to the reservation," said Marcel.

"Take them to the office. Grey Dove is there, and she can help them get signed in."

"Thank you, Principal Leopard," said Marcel.

Marcel led the way to the office. He opened the door and entered without knocking. Grey Dove looked up and smiled when she recognized Marcel.

"Good morning, Marcel. I haven't seen you in a while. I have sign-in papers all ready. If the parents will fill them in, we can get started," said Grey Dove.

"How did you know we were going to need sign-in papers?" asked Marcel.

"I ran into Moon Walking yesterday, and she told me to have them ready," said Grey Dove.

Marcel smiled. "It's nice to know Moon Walking is looking out for us."

"Yes," agreed Grey Dove.

Lanie had been listening to their conversation while she filled out Chris's registration. She had a lot of questions, starting with who Moon Walking was.

"Is there a bus running out at Dancing Eagle's old place?" asked Marcel.

"We had a bus driver to go around and pick up children in out of the way places, places not on a regular route. But he had to quit because of health problems, and we haven't found anyone to take his place," said Grey Dove.

"Didn't you drive a delivery truck?" Marcel asked Randell.

"Yes, I did. It was part-time," said Randell.

"You should have a commercial license," said Marcel.

"Yes, I do," agreed Randell.

"You could drive the bus and pick up the hard-to-get-to students," said Marcel.

"What about my job with you?" asked Randell.

"You would still be working for me. You can check fences and keep an eye out for rustlers in between running the bus route," said Marcel.

Randell grinned. "I would like to try," he said.

Grey Dove handed him an application. "Just fill this out," she said.

Marcel grinned. "Let me guess, Moon Walking told you to have an application ready," said Marcel.

Grey Dove smiled. "Yes, she did." Grey Dove took the children's registrations from their parents and looked them over. "Chris and Nick, you'll be in my class. Joy, you will be in the fourth grade. Susan Sparrow will be your teacher. I'll send off after all of your records today. We should have them back in a few days. If you will take a seat, I'll take you to your classes in a few minutes. Did you bring lunches?"

"I packed Chris one. I didn't know what was available here," said Lanie.

"We have a lunchroom, but anyone can bring lunches if they want to," said Grey Dove.

Marcel drew out his wallet and handed Grey Dove some money. "Sign them all up for lunches. When this runs out, let me know."

Grey Dove took the money and made a note of it in a book on the desk. She then put the money in a drawer. She accepted Randell's application and looked it over. "I'll have a bus assigned to you, and we will work up a route for you. I'll have someone ride with you to show you around until you become familiar with the route." She went to the intercom and pressed a button. "Gary Fox, will you report to the office, please?"

"Gary is a twelfth grader. He can ride the route with you in the morning and after school until you learn your way around."

Gary came into the office. "You sent for me, Miss Dove?" he asked.

"Yes, Gary, this is Mr. Stavos. He is going to be taking Leny Wolf's old route. I would like for you to ride with him and show him the route. He is new to the reservation and is living in Dancing Eagle's house, so it will take a while for him to know his way around. Will you help us?" asked Grey Dove.

"Sure," agreed Gary.

"We will get Mr. Stavos set up with a bus, and he can start the route tomorrow."

"I'll have Milo pick you up and take you to pick up the bus this afternoon. You can have the bus at your house to start the route tomorrow morning. Milo can show you where Gary lives so you can pick him up first," said Marcel. "Grey Dove can announce the bus will be picking up students so they will not need rides in the morning."

Grey Dove rose and motioned for the students to go with her.

43

Chris, Nick, and Joy rose and followed her after quick grins to their mothers. Gary said goodbye and left for class.

"When you pick up your bus, you can pick up Joy and Nick," said Marcel. He turned to Lanie. "Joey is going to make sure Chris gets on the bus with him."

"Okay," said Lanie with a nod. "Do we leave now?"

Marcel laughed. "Yes, we can leave now. We need to get out of their way so they can start their day," said Marcel. All of the students had been greeting Marcel as they passed on the way to their classes.

When they got outside and entered the SUV, Lanie sighed. "This place is quite an experience," she said.

Marcel smiled. "Good or bad?" he asked.

"Good, definitely good," assured Lanie. Randell and Merry agreed with her from the back seat.

Marcel patted her leg and went on his way to take Randell and Merry home. When he dropped them off, they both thanked Marcel again for all of his help.

"When people need help, the Great Spirit says help them as you would want someone to help you," said Marcel.

"I will always remember to follow that rule," said Randell.

Lanie waved goodbye, and they headed for home. Before they turned to the road to their home, Marcel asked Lanie if she would like to look around Rolling Fork.

"Sure, if you don't need to get back," said Lanie.

"It won't take long. It's not far. I want you to see there is a very good shopping place when you can't find what you want on the reservation," said Marcel. Marcel called Milo and asked him to pick Randell up and take him to pick up his bus and to show him where Gary Fox lived.

"Sure, Boss, I'll pick him up after lunch," said Milo.

"Thanks, Milo," said Marcel as he hung up his phone.

Marcel drove around Rolling Fork and pointed out different places to Lanie. He showed her the park. He drove by the Gallery and pointed out other stores on the street. As he drove by the police station, Mark drove up and stopped beside him.

"Hello," said Mark. "Is something wrong?"

"No, I was just showing Lanie around Rolling Fork," said Marcel. He looked over and saw Gunner sitting in Mark's car.

"Hi, Gunner, you planning on joining the police force?" asked Marcel. Gunner got out of the car and came around to stand beside Marcel's car.

"I'm thinking about it. The captain wants me to ride along with Mark for a few days. I think Brenda and I are ready to move to Rolling Fork. With May and April here, there is no reason to go back to Baron. I think working with Rolling Fork Police Department might suit me fine," said Gunner.

"I think it's a great idea. If you need any help, just let any of us know. We would love to have you and Brenda stay here," said Marcel.

"Thanks," said Gunner. "Mark has already offered. It is great to find such good friends."

"You won't find better people anywhere," said Lanie.

Marcel smiled. "Gunner, this is Lanie Melton. She is new here, too. She is my new housekeeper," said Marcel. "Lanie, meet Gunner Merril. His sister May married our cousin Silas Light Feather and Gunner's sister April married Silas's brother Jamie. Silas and May own the property where the Stavos family is living."

"It's nice to meet you, Gunner. I'm looking forward to meeting your sisters," said Lanie.

"It's nice to meet you. I'm sure May and April will be looking forward to meeting you. I imagine they have already heard all about you from Doris and Willow."

They all laughed their agreement with Gunner's statement, which they knew was probably true. Mark and Gunner left to go inside, and Marcel and Lanie drove on.

CHAPTER 6

*M*arcel drove around, showing Lanie more places of interest.

"This is all fine," said Lanie. "But I would like to see more of the reservation."

Marcel smiled and turned and headed for home. Lanie sat back and enjoyed the ride. It wasn't far, but it was beautiful country. She looked around, enjoying the view.

They drove by the Community Center. "Is this where they play bingo?" asked Lanie.

"Yes, every Thursday," said Marcel.

"Your mom asked Sally to go; she loves bingo," said Lanie.

"She will make a lot of friends there," said Marcel.

"Good," said Lanie.

Marcel drove down the main street, pointing out stores and offices. Next, he drove by the school and pointed out the new sports complex. He explained that the sports complex was built by the Black Foundation and was named after Angelica's mother.

"It is called the Shining Star Sports Complex," said Marcel.

"It's a wonderful tribute," said Lanie.

"Yes," agreed Marcel. "My brother's and I take turns going in and mentoring the boys and girls at the sports complex. We are there to play sports with them or to talk to them if they need to talk. We think it is important for our young people to be shown encouragement and guidance."

"It is very important," agreed Lanie. She was looking at Marcel with love and admiration in her eyes. She was learning more about this amazing man. It was hard to believe such a wonderful person was still single, but she was glad he was.

Marcel smiled and headed for home. "I know you are going to be anxious until Chris gets off his bus, but try not to worry too much. Remember, Joey will be with him, and everyone on the reservation knows Joey, and they know he is a Black Feather. He will be fine," said Marcel.

"I know you are right," said Lanie as they stopped in front of the house.

"I will be in later," said Marcel. "I have three horses about ready to foal, and I need to check on them."

"Okay," said Lanie. She turned and went inside, and Marcel drove his car around to the garage and headed for the barn.

The horses were fine and, after checking and talking to each horse, Marcel headed for the house.

He found Lanie in the kitchen trying to decide what to fix for supper. Marcel came up behind her, and, standing close, he peered over her shoulder. "Isn't it a little early to worry about supper?" asked Marcel.

"I was looking to see what was available," said Lanie.

Marcel closed the pantry door and took Lanie's hand to lead her to the front porch. He led her over to the porch swing and drew her down beside him. Marcel looked down at Lanie and smiled. She smiled back at him and enjoyed feeling his arm across the back of the swing over her shoulders.

"We can sit here and enjoy the nice day while we watch for the bus," said Marcel.

47

"This is nice," said Lanie as she leaned back into Marcel's touch.

Marcel agreed, but he didn't say anything. He was savoring Lanie's closeness. They sat there quietly, enjoying each other's company and the feelings they had for each other. The feelings were growing stronger the more they were around each other.

Milo drove up into the yard and came over to the porch. "Mr. Stavos has picked up his bus. I showed him where Gary lives, and I followed him home to make sure he knew the way," said Milo.

"Thanks, Milo," said Marcel.

"Hi, Milo," said Lanie.

"Miss Lanie," said Milo, nodding.

"Mrs. Black Feather suggested you might bring Sally to bingo with you Thursday," said Lanie.

"Sure," said Milo. "I'll be pleased to."

"Thanks, I'll tell Sally," said Lanie. Milo smiled and went to move his car. Lanie smiled up at Marcel. "I want Sally to be happy here," said Lanie.

"She will be. She will have a lot more freedom than she had in Liberty. She can get out and do things in the community. I think my mom is taking an interest in her. Mom will help her get to know people and to make friends," said Marcel.

"Yes, I think so, too. They seemed to really have taken a liking to each other," said Lanie. "I have been meaning to ask you something."

"What?" asked Marcel.

"Who is Moon Walking?" asked Lanie.

Marcel smiled. "Moon Walking is a Tribal Elder. She is also a Wise Woman. She keeps an eye on all of us and makes sure we are prepared for most situations. When Moon Walking tells us something, we listen. She always knows what is going to happen, and she helps us to be prepared. She is always one step ahead. Her grandson is Dr. Alex Steel, Angelica's husband. Angelica and Alex are both great at helping out the reservation."

"Wow," said Lanie. "I can't wait to meet her."

"You will meet her when Moon Walking has some news for you," said Marcel.

"Maybe I shouldn't be in a hurry to meet her," said Lanie.

Marcel laughed. "Don't worry," he said, giving her shoulder a squeeze.

Lanie settled back into his arm to enjoy his touch. Lanie and Marcel sat up and watched as Dawn's car stopped in front of the house. Dawn got out and opened the passenger door for Moon Walking. Marcel and Lanie came to meet them as Dawn helped Moon Walking up the steps to the porch.

"Hello, Moon Walking," said Marcel as he took her hand and helped her to a chair.

"Thank you," said Moon Walking. "I asked your sister to bring me to your house because I wished to warn the new member of our community."

Lanie came forward and took Moon Walking's hand. "I'm very pleased to meet you. I'm Lanie."

Moon Walking smiled. She squeezed Lanie's hand. "I am very happy you have joined the Black Feather family, Lanie. You are a welcome addition."

"What did you want to warn me about?" asked Lanie.

Moon Walking stared into Lanie's eyes for a minute before speaking. Lanie waited patiently. "There are stormy times ahead, but as long as you depend on your new family, you will weather the storms. It is good you have taken love's gamble. Do not be afraid of gambling on love, because when you do, you will always be a winner." Moon Walking smiled at Lanie and seemed relieved to have delivered her message.

"Thank you, Moon Walking, for bringing me the message. I will remember everything you have told me," said Lanie.

"You are a sweet child. Could I have a glass of tea before Dawn takes me back to town?" asked Moon Walking.

"Of course," said Lanie, flushing slightly. "I should have offered. I'll be right back." She hurried inside to get the requested tea.

After drinking the tea, Lanie had fetched for her, Moon Walking took Marcel's arm and let him escort her to Dawn's car. Lanie followed them out to the car, and they all waved goodbye. Lanie and Marcel went back to the porch and sat in the swing. Lanie's mind was working to fast to relax.

"What did she mean about storms?" asked Lanie.

"I don't know. I would think she meant some type of trouble. I guess we will have to wait and see but be on guard," said Marcel.

"I can understand about the gamble we took leaving Liberty and coming here. I'm glad she said it was a winning solution," said Lanie.

Marcel smiled. He didn't think Moon Walking was talking about the move at all, but if Lanie was happy with her interpretation, he wasn't saying anything, yet.

"Don't worry. We are all here for you. If you have any trouble, let me know. We will handle it together," said Marcel.

A few minutes later, the school bus pulled to a stop and let Chris off. He ran to the porch before turning and waving to Joey and some other new friends. Joey lowered his window and yelled. "Hello, Uncle Marcel."

Lanie and Marcel laughed and waved. They heard the bus driver say, "Put that window up, young Black Feather." Joey raised the window but continued to wave while the bus turned and headed for the road.

Lanie noticed the hand full of papers Chris had and took them as she led him inside. "Did you have a good day?" asked Lanie.

"It was great," said Chris. "I am so glad we moved." Marcel smiled as he watched Lanie and Chris go inside. He was glad they had moved, too.

Lanie sent Chris to change clothes while she made him a snack before he did his homework. She made him a peanut butter and jelly sandwich and added a glass of milk. When Chris came back from changing, he sat down and devoured it happily. It was his favorite afterschool snack.

Lanie had been looking at the papers Chris brought home. It was all pretty basic stuff. Most of it was just information they had already covered at school when Chris was registered. There was a question mark beside the request for his records to be transferred. She would have to call and see what it was about. After Chris finished eating, he quickly did his homework.

"Will Marcel be able to show me the horses today?" asked Chris.

"I don't know. Let's go ask him," said Lanie.

They went out to the porch to find Marcel still sitting in the porch swing, relaxing and thinking about Moon Walking's visit. When Lanie and Chris came onto the porch, Marcel looked up with a smile.

"Chris was wondering if you had time to introduce him to some horses," said Lanie.

"I was about to go and check on the horses in the barn. Would you both like to meet our soon-to-be mamas?" asked Marcel. Both Lanie and Chris nodded their heads happily.

Marcel laughed and, rising, took Lanie's hand and led the way to the barn. When they entered the barn, Marcel turned on the light and led the way to the stalls with the horses in them. At the first stall, the horse stuck her head over the door and rooted around for a treat. Marcel handed a piece of carrot to Chris and showed him how to hold his hand for the horse to take it. Chris smiled delightedly as the horse delicately took the carrot from his hand.

Marcel patted the horse and talked to her while he was looking her over. Deciding she was okay, they went on to the next stall where they repeated the process. Lanie watched as Chris proudly fed each of the horses and patted them like Marcel was doing. It looked like the horses loved the attention. After checking all three horses, they went outside to stand at the fence and watch Stanley ride through the horses in the pasture. He was on his way back from checking the fence in one of the pastures. Stanley pulled to a stop in front of them and smiled down at the group.

"How did it go?" asked Marcel.

"Everything is fine. I found one small spot, but I fixed it before it could get bigger. I'll keep an eye on it for a few days to be sure it holds," said Stanley.

"Good," agreed Marcel.

"I need to go and start supper," said Lanie.

"You can leave Chris with me. I'll bring him in later," said Marcel.

"Okay," said Lanie. "If he gets in the way, send him inside." Lanie turned and went inside, leaving Chris happily with his new friends, the horses.

"Chris, do you know the number one rule on the ranch?" asked Marcel.

Chris nodded his head. "Always close the gate. Joey told me."

"Good, did he tell you why?" asked Marcel. Chris shook his head. "It is because if the gate is left open, the horses may get out. They could get hurt or stolen," said Marcel.

"I'll remember," promised Chris.

Marcel rubbed his head. "I know you will," he said.

Chris beamed with pride.

CHAPTER 7

*M*arcel walked around to the treehouse with Chris. He wanted to check on it to be sure it was still in good shape. He knew the boys would be playing in it anytime they got the chance.

He and Chris climbed the steps and entered the door. Marcel looked around and checked for leaks. Everything seemed to be okay. There were some toys and board games there. They were all neatly put away, waiting to be played with again. All of the children knew to put things away before they left when playing in the treehouse. They left, and Marcel made sure the door was tightly closed before they climbed down.

When they were back on the ground, they headed for the house. As soon as they went inside, they smelled a nice aroma coming from the kitchen. "Mom is making supper," said Chris with a grin.

"Let's get washed up so we will be ready when she calls us," said Marcel.

Marcel and Chris went and washed their hands. They then went to the dining room, and Marcel offered to set the table, with Chris's help, while they were waiting.

Lanie smiled and agreed. She was making meatballs in gravy, mashed potatoes, green beans, and corn. She had apple pie for dessert. "It's almost ready," she said. "Sally made the apple pie earlier." Lanie started putting food on the table, and Marcel filled glasses with iced tea. "Chris, go let Sally know supper is ready," said Lanie.

"Okay, Mom," said Chris. He went to their apartment to let Sally know they were ready to eat.

Sally came with Chris and sniffed as she came into the dining room. "It smells good," said Sally.

Lanie smiled. "Everyone sit, and we will see if it tastes as good as it smells."

Marcel seated Sally and then Lanie before taking his chair. When they were seated, they all held hands, and Marcel said a blessing before they ate. Marcel and Chris were talking about the horses. Mostly, Chris was asking questions, and Marcel was answering them patiently. Sally and Lanie smiled and listened indulgently.

All the plates were cleared, and everyone helped clear the table while Lanie put the dishes in the dishwasher. Sally took Chris into their apartment to watch television for a short while before bedtime.

Marcel took Lanie's hand and led her to the front porch and the swing. Once there, he sat and pulled her down and held her close while they watched the stars and enjoyed the night. Lanie lay back into Marcel's arms with a sigh.

"You are not cold, are you?" asked Marcel.

"No, the air feels great. You have a beautiful place here," said Lanie.

"So, you're not sorry you came here with me," remarked Marcel.

"No, it was the best decision I have ever made," assured Lanie.

Marcel tightened his arms around her slightly. She had not objected to him holding her this way.

"You know I did not bring you here just because I needed a housekeeper," said Marcel.

Lanie looked at him and smiled. "You didn't," she whispered.

"No, I needed a housekeeper, but I took one look at you and knew I was fated to love you. When we touched and were shocked, I knew you were meant for me," said Marcel.

"What does being shocked have to do with anything?" asked Lanie.

"It usually happens when couples meet through the magic mirror, but sometimes when there is a strong connection, a couple will be shocked when they touch when first meeting," said Marcel.

"What's a magic mirror?" asked Lanie.

"You have never heard of the magic mirror?" asked Marcel.

"No," said Lanie.

"There are several, but we have one in The Gallery in Rolling Fork. When women look in the mirror, it will sometimes show them their true love," said Marcel. Lanie looked at him skeptically. "It really happens," assured Marcel. "You remember May and Silas?" Lanie nodded. "They had seen each other when they were children. Then May's family moved away, and they didn't see each other for ten years. One day, May looked in the magic mirror in Sharpville and saw Silas. They recognized each other at once, and Silas went to Barons where she was living and brought her home with him."

"Wow," said Lanie. "What a wonderful legacy to pass down to their children," said Lanie.

"Yes, but I didn't need a magic mirror to know you and I belonged together," said Marcel. "I felt it in my heart from the time we met. Fate was with us, helping us along. It made your car break down and gave me an excuse to load you up and bring you home with me. It gave us a chance to get to know each other so you could realize what I already knew. We are meant to be a family."

Marcel leaned forward and kissed her gently. Lanie accepted his kiss and savored it. It gave her tingly feelings all the way to her toes. Marcel looked at Lanie to see if she had any objections. When she smiled, he drew a breath of relief. He had been afraid he was acting too soon, but he felt he had to be honest with her about his feelings. He didn't object to going slow. He just wanted Lanie to know they were going to be together. He gathered her close in his arms and held her while they both savored the closeness.

After a while, Lanie stirred and looked up at Marcel. "I need to go and tell Chris good night," she said. Marcel stood and, holding her hand, helped her to her feet and went with her to tell Chris good night. Chris was already in bed. He smiled up at his mom and Marcel.

"Good night, Chris," said Marcel.

"Good night, thanks for letting me feed the horses," said Chris.

"Sure thing," said Marcel with a smile.

"Good night, sweetie," said Lanie as she leaned over and kissed Chris on the top of his head. "I'll see you in the morning."

"Good night, Mom," said Chris.

Lanie turned out the light and left the door open a bit so Chris would get some light. They went back through the living room and said goodnight to Sally before going into the main part of the house.

Sally looked at their joined hands and smiled. Everything was going to work out fine, she thought.

The next morning, while Chris was eating his breakfast, Lanie remembered the paper he had brought home the day before. She called the office at the school.

"Hello, Grey Dove speaking, how can I help you?"

"Hello, Grey Dove, this is Lanie Melton. I registered my son Chris yesterday for school."

"Yes, how can I help you, Mrs. Melton?" asked Grey Dove.

"When Chris brought home some papers yesterday, there was a question mark beside his school records. Is there a problem?" asked Lanie.

"When we sent a request for his records, we were informed a hold had been placed on his records," said Grey Dove.

"A hold? Why would there be a hold on his records?" asked Lanie.

"It's possible it could be as simple as some unfinished work," said Grey Dove. "You will have to check with the school. When you have it straightened out, please ask them to send the records on to us as we requested."

"I'll do that," said Lanie. "I will let you know what I find out."

"Thank you. Moon Walking told us to keep Chris in class. She said everything will be straightened out," said Grey Dove.

"I'm sure everything will be fine," said Lanie. They both hung up, and Lanie called the school in Liberty.

"Hello, Liberty Elementary," said a voice.

"This is Lanie Melton. My son, Christopher, and I moved, and when I registered him in his new school, the school sent to you for his school records yesterday. They were told there was a hold put on his records. Could you tell me why a hold would be placed on the records of a second-grader?" asked Lanie.

Marcel had come in the back door and was standing listening to Lanie talk to the school. Chris was also listening.

"Mrs. Melton. I have Christopher's records here. There was a court-ordered hold placed on his records by Timothy and Gladys Melton."

"What!?" exclaimed Lanie. "What right do Timothy and Gladys Melton have to put a hold on my son's school records?" asked Lanie.

"I'm sorry, but I don't know the answer to your question. You need to talk to a lawyer," said the person she was talking to.

Lanie hung up the phone and sat down, stunned. She looked up at Marcel. "How could Ben's parents do something like this?" she asked.

Marcel pulled her into his arms. "Let's get Chris ready for the bus, and we will go talk to Dad," said Marcel.

"Am I going to be able to go to my new school?" asked Chris.

Lanie went to him and hugged him. "Of course you are. This is just a misunderstanding. I'll get it straightened out." Lanie tried to show a happy face for Chris, but she was worried. Why were Timothy and Gladys coming around after all of this time?

She and Marcel did not talk about the situation while they helped Chris get ready to catch the bus. When they heard the horn blow, they hurried Chris out to catch the bus. He looked much happier when he sat beside Joey and they were on their way to school.

Lanie went inside and asked Sally to straighten the kitchen and told her what was going on. Then she and Marcel left to go and talk to Glen Black Feather.

They were met in the office by April Light Feather, Glen's intern and their cousin Jamie Light Feather's wife.

"Hi, April," said Marcel. "This is Lanie Melton. We need to talk to Dad."

"Hello, Marcel. It's nice to meet you, Mrs. Melton," said April.

"Call me Lanie, please. It's nice to meet you, too," said Lanie.

April went and knocked on Glen's door. "Marcel and Lanie are here to see you," said April as she opened the door to Glen's come in.

Glen rose and came around his desk to greet Marcel and Lanie. "Is anything wrong?" he asked.

"I found out Ben's parents got a court order to put a hold on Chris's school records," said Lanie.

Glen nodded.

"You don't look surprised," said Marcel. "What's going on?"

"I received a report back from Angelica. She had the Black Foundation do some checking on the group planning to build the condos in Liberty. She thought it was strange when she found Timothy and Gladys Melton on the board of directors of the group." Lanie gasped. Glen nodded. "They were the instigators for the entire thing. The condos were their idea, and they sent out the eviction notices."

"But, why?" asked Lanie.

"They wanted you vulnerable. They wanted to make sure you had nowhere to turn when they went after custody of Chris," said Glen.

Lanie sat in her chair, stunned. Marcel put an arm around her shoulder.

"Have they ever met Chris?" asked Glen.

"No, they moved away from Liberty the day after we buried Ben.

They did not tell me where they were moving to. When Chris was born, I wrote them a letter and told them about him. I sent it to their old address there in Liberty. I thought it might be forwarded. It didn't come back, but I don't know if they got it. They never got in touch with me. So, they have never met Chris."

"They were willing to put two dozen families out of their homes just to try and steal Chris from Lanie," said Marcel.

"Yes," agreed Glen.

"They would have felt the people in the subdivision were beneath their notice. They felt like poor people got what they deserved. It would not have mattered to them at all. Ben was not like them," said Lanie.

"I'm sure if they have gone so far as to put a hold on Chris's school records, they have probably filed in court to take custody of Chris," said Glen. "We just haven't received the notice."

Lanie gasped and went pale. Marcel squeezed her hand.

"It will be alright," he said. "We have advanced warning."

"Yes, we do," agreed Glen. "We will be ready for them."

"What are we going to do?" asked Lanie.

"Are you hiring me as your lawyer?" asked Glen.

"I can't afford to hire you," stammered Lanie.

"Do you have a dollar?" asked Glen.

"Yes." Lanie opened her purse and took out a dollar and handed it to Glen.

"I am officially your lawyer. The Meltons' lawyer can not force me to talk about your case," said Glen.

Marcel smiled and gave Lanie's hand a squeeze.

"Now," said Glen. I need to talk to Judge Hawthorn and get him to talk to the governor about the Meltons' business practices. There are laws against throwing people out of their homes without helping them find another place to live. By the time we are through with the Meltons, they may be looking for a place to live," said Glen with satisfaction. "Don't worry, Lanie. The Meltons have no chance of getting Chris away from you. We may have to make a court appearance, but I promise you they have no case," said Glen. "Now, you let Marcel take you out for coffee and let me get to work."

Marcel rose and helped Lanie to stand while keeping an arm around her.

"Thank you, Glen. I'm glad you are on my side," said Lanie.

"Yes, thanks, Dad," said Marcel. He shook Glen's hand and guided Lanie out of the office.

Glen smiled after they left and called Judge Hawthorn. There was nothing he liked better than giving payback to people like the Meltons, and Judge Hawthorn felt the same way. They were going to enjoy showing the Meltons a little of what they had been putting out.

CHAPTER 8

"*H*ello, this is Glen Black Feather. Would it be possible for me to speak with Judge Hawthorn?"

"Hold, please, I'll check." Glen waited patiently for an answer.

"Hello, Glen, how are you?" asked Judge Hawthorn.

"I am doing good, Judge. How is your family doing? I heard you had a new grandson."

"Yes, Dora has presented us with another grandson. We are headed to Morristown this weekend to see him. As a matter of fact, the governor is going with us. He wants to meet his new Godson," said the Judge. "Now, we have all of that out of the way, you can tell me what's on your mind," said the Judge.

Glen laughed. "I can't get anything past you," said Glen. "I'm calling you about a group of investors in Liberty. They bought up a housing complex and are tearing the houses down and building condos. There were about two dozen families living there, and they were sent notices to get out in a week or be evicted. They had no advanced notice of anything and were completely blindsided. I called Angelica, and the Black Foundation has found places for most of the families, and they are working on the others."

"It sounds as if you are taking care of them. Why are you calling me?" asked the Judge.

"I'm calling you because my son Marcel is involved with one of the residents of the housing complex. He arrived there and rescued her and brought her to the reservation with him. The Black Foundation found out that Lanie's former in-laws, Timothy and Gladys Melton, are behind the evictions. They were trying to put Lanie in a position where they could take her seven-year-old son away from her. We just found out about all of this today. When Lanie registered her son in school, she found out the Meltons had put a freeze on his school records."

"They can't do that," said the Judge.

"I know, but they did," said Glen. "I was wondering if the Attorney General could do something about the Meltons and maybe have those families compensated," said Glen.

"I'll see what I can do. Tell me Lanie's and her son's full names, and I will see to those school records. They had no right to hold those records. I want to find out which judge was stupid enough to sign off on such a thing." said the Judge.

"Their names are Delaney Melton and Christopher Melton. Chris's father was killed in the Army almost eight years ago. His parents moved away after the funeral and didn't tell Lanie their new address. They have never met Chris," said Glen.

"Tell Lanie the records will be there today. Give her and Marcel my best wishes. We need to get together for a visit after we get back from Morristown. Thanks for letting me know what was going on, Glen."

The Judge hung up and looked at the Governor. "Well, since I had the phone on speaker, I assume you got most of what he was talking about," said the Judge.

The Governor nodded. He took out his phone and called the Attorney General's office. He gave them the information and told them he wanted someone out there investigating today. He told them to check with the Black Foundation to save time on the investigation.

After he hung up, the Judge had his secretary call the elementary school in Liberty.

"Hello, this is Judge Hawthorn from Rolling Fork. I want to speak to the principal."

Just a minute later, the principal was on the line. "How can I help you, Judge Hawthorn?" asked the principal.

"You can tell me what judge signed an order to put a hold on Christopher Melton's school records," said the Judge.

The principal pulled up Christopher Melton's records. "It was Judge Salkow in Kansas City," said the principal.

"I see. This judge's ruling is overturned. He had no authority to make the ruling in the first place. You are to forward the records at once to the reservation school requesting them." said the Judge.

"I can't do that," said the principal. "Not without written authorization."

"How about approval from the governor?" asked the Judge. He handed the phone to the governor.

"This is the Governor. Do you have a fax in your office?"

"Yes, Sir," stammered the principal.

"Give me your number, and I'll have authorization faxed to you at once. Make sure you forward those records." The Governor wrote down the number as the principal gave it to him. "Before you hold back anyone else's records, make sure to check it out," said the Governor.

"Yes, Sir, I will," said the principal, but he was talking to a silent phone. The Governor had hung up.

"Have your secretary type up a paper for me to sign and fax it to the number here," said the Governor handing the number to the Judge.

The Judge grinned as he gave the information to his secretary. She had the paper ready for the Governor to sign in a minute. As soon as he signed it, she faxed it to the school in Liberty.

The Judge and the Governor chuckled as they left the courthouse and headed for the Judge's house. "I do enjoy a slight confrontation once in a while," said the Governor.

Glen Black Feather was smiling as he left his office and started for home. Marcel and Lanie were sitting on the porch. The bus had already dropped Chris off, and he had a snack. Sally was watching him do his homework. Marcel had his arm around Lanie, holding her close to his side. When Glen pulled up, Lanie tensed up, but when she saw he was smiling, she relaxed.

"Hi, Dad," said Marcel. "Is there any news?"

"Yes, there is. I talked to Judge Hawthorn, and Chris's records will be at the school today. Judge Hawthorn is going to have the Meltons and the rest of the investors in the condos investigated by the Attorney General's office. I have a feeling the Meltons are going to be so busy getting out of trouble they won't have time to try anything else, but if they do, they will have to come here and appear before Judge Hawthorn, and he will be ready for them. So, don't worry," said Glen.

Lanie stood up and went over and gave Glen a hug. "Thank you," she said.

Marcel smiled. "Yes, thank you, Dad," he said.

"I have to get home. Your mom will be expecting me. I just wanted to let you know what was happening," said Glen. He headed for his car and waved as he left.

Marcel pulled Lanie close in his arms. "I told you there was nothing to worry about. I knew Dad could handle it," he said.

Lanie laughed, and, looking up, she leaned up and kissed him. Marcel was startled at first, then he deepened the kiss. They didn't stop until they had to breathe and Marcel heard Chris coming outside.

He settled himself and Lanie in the swing and kept her close to his side while he greeted Chris. Chris came over and sat in the swing next to Lanie. Lanie put an arm around him and gave him a hug. Marcel ruffled his hair. Chris grinned at them. He had never been part of a family group that included a male. It had always been him, his Mom, and Sally. He enjoyed having the male attention.

"Did you finish your homework?" asked Lanie.

"Yes, Ma'am," said Chris.

"Mr. Glen arranged for your school records to be unfrozen, and they will be sent to your new school today or in the morning," said Lanie.

"Alright," said Chris with a big grin.

"Why did my dad's parents try to cause trouble?" asked Chris. "Why didn't they ever try to come and see me?"

"I'm not sure they knew about you at first," said Lanie. "They moved away after your dad died, and I didn't know where they were. I tried to write them, but I don't know if they received my letter. They are trying to make trouble because they blame me for your dad's death."

"But he died in the army," said Chris.

"Yes, he did, but they believed if it hadn't been for me, he would have stayed home and gone to college instead of joining the army. What they didn't know, because your dad never told them, was your dad was recruited for the army when he was in the tenth grade. The recruiter told him he would be back for him in two years. Your dad and I were not seeing each other until the eleventh grade, but he always told me he was going to join the army when he graduated. When he came home after basic training, he persuaded me to marry him before he shipped out to go overseas. He was only over there two weeks when he was killed by sniper fire. His parents were looking for someone to blame, and I was an easy target."

"It's okay, Mom. We don't need them. We have Sally, and now we have Marcel," said Chris.

Chris smiled at Marcel, and Marcel smiled back at him. "Yes, you do, I'm going to be here for you and your mom anytime you need me," agreed Marcel. "Do you want to go with me to check on the ladies?" asked Marcel.

"Can I, Mom?" asked Chris with a grin

"Okay, but, as soon as you get back, you will take your bath and get ready for bed," said Lanie.

"I will," promised Chris as he took Marcel's hand to go to the barn with him.

They were back in just a little while, and Marcel left Chris with Lanie and hurried back out. He took out his phone and called Stanley.

"One of our ladies has gone into labor," he told Stanley.

"I'll be right there," said Stanley.

Stanley hurried over and met Marcel in the barn. He was anxiously looking over the mare. Stanley gave her a quick once over. "I think she is doing fine," said Stanley.

"Yes," agreed Marcel. "She looks like she is handling it like a pro."

"Just keep sweet-talking her to keep her calm," said Stanley with a smile.

"You can laugh, but it works," said Marcel with a smile as he went to the mare's head and started patting her head and talking to her. The mare listened to his voice and was much calmer. About two hours later, she delivered a healthy foal. Mother and baby were doing fine.

Marcel tiredly made his way to the house to find Lanie waiting for him in the kitchen. She had made him a plate and kept it warm for him. "You didn't have to wait up for me," said Marcel as he washed his hands. He turned to Lanie and drew her into his arms. "I am glad you did," he said as he kissed her.

"How is the mare?" asked Lanie when he stopped for breath.

"Mother and baby are doing great. The foal was already nursing when I left the barn. Stanley is going to keep a check on them tonight," said Marcel.

"Sit down. I'll get your plate. Do you want tea or water?" asked Lanie.

"Water is fine," said Marcel. "Sit with me while I eat. I need to unwind before trying to sleep."

Marcel said a brief prayer, thanking the Great Spirit for a healthy foal, before digging into his food.

"When you were telling Chris about his Dad earlier, I realized you were hardly a bride before you were a widow," said Marcel.

"I didn't feel much like a bride," said Lanie. "Ben died, and then my dad died, and my brother took my mother away, and I felt so alone and scared. I was only eighteen. Sally was a Godsend. She is like a grandmother to me as much as she is to Chris. She stood by us and helped every way she could. I owe her my very sanity," said Lanie.

"We are going to have to do something nice for her," said Marcel.

"What?" asked Lanie.

"I don't know, but I'll think of something," said Marcel. "Right now, I just want to kiss my lady."

"Your lady would like that very much," said Lanie.

Marcel held her close and kissed her. When he pulled back, he grinned at Lanie. "Do you know this is the first time you have admitted to being my lady," said Marcel.

Lanie smiled. "I guess I have to admit it. I am becoming addicted to your kisses," said Lanie.

"I'm glad," said Marcel. "I have already turned my heart over to you. It is in your keeping. Treat it gently."

"I will. I never want to do anything to cause any ache in your heart, because when your heart aches, mine aches," said Lanie.

Needless to say, they didn't come up for air anytime soon.

The next morning, Chris was very excited about the new foal. Marcel took him to the barn so he could see the foal before leaving for school. He could hardly wait for the bus so he could tell Joey all about her.

Lanie laughed as she watched Chris hurry to the bus, and she saw him start talking before he even sat down.

Marcel was down at the barn, so Lanie went inside to clean the kitchen and do some house cleaning. She was also determined to do some laundry today. There had been so much happening since they had come to the reservation. She had not established a routine.

Even though she and Marcel were getting closer, she was going to do the job she had come here to do. She was not going to take advantage of the feelings between Marcel and herself.

Lanie cleaned the kitchen and set the dishwasher to running. She then went to Marcel's room and took his dirty clothes basket and started the washer to working. She went back to Marcel's room and stripped his bed and remade it with clean sheets from the linen closet. She took the bedclothes to the washroom to be washed next. She got a bucket of pine-scented water and mopped the floor in Marcel's room and on down the hall into the living room. After she switched the clothes to the dryer, she put the bedclothes in to wash. Satisfied with the work she had done so far, Lanie started mopping the kitchen and dining room.

Marcel started to come in the back door but stopped when he saw Lanie mopping.

"You can go around front," said Lanie. "The living room should be dry by now."

"I'll just go back out to the barn. I don't want to track up the floors before they dry," said Marcel, backing up.

Lanie grinned at him. "Okay," she said.

Marcel looked like he wanted to say something, but he changed his mind. He turned and went back outside. Lanie looked after him, curious as to what he had been going to say. She shrugged her shoulder and finished the floor.

She went into the apartment and gathered all of their dirty clothes and took them to the laundry room to be washed. While she was there, she took Marcel's clothes out of the dryer and put the bedclothes in. After putting their clothes in to wash, she took Marcel's clothes to be put away.

She went into his room and found hangers to hang all of his shirts and pants in the closet. The socks and underwear she folded and left on the bed for him to put away.

Satisfied, Lanie went to see what to do next. She felt good. It was nice to be busy doing the job she had promised to do. It gave her a good feeling. She was used to being busy. Having too much spare time made her feel weird.

Lanie turned and smiled at Sally. She had been down at the barn with Milo. He had been showing her the new foal and making plans with her for bingo on Thursday. Sally looked flushed with excitement when she came in. She looked around and sniffed.

"It smells great in here. I see you have been busy," said Sally.

"Yes, I thought it was time for me to do the job Marcel is paying me to do," said Lanie.

Sally looked at her strangely. "You do know Marcel didn't bring us here because of a job," she said.

CHAPTER 9

"I know," agreed Lanie with a smile. "I have feelings for him too, but, until things change and maybe after they change, this is my home, and I want it to be taken care of."

"Good for you," said Sally. She came over and gave Lanie a hug. "The new foal is precious. I could just stare at her for ages. She is so delicate but strong at the same time. You need to go down and see her when you are through cleaning."

"Maybe I will," said Lanie. She heard a ping and went to unload the dryer and put a new load in to dry. She folded the sheets and put them in the hall linen closet. While she was waiting for the last load to dry, Lanie went and looked around to see what she could prepare to eat.

She braised some meat and put it in a large pot with some potatoes and onions and other vegetables. After adding water, she put it on a low heat to simmer slowly. Before closing the lid, she added some salt and butter. She went and took the laundry from the dryer and carried it to her apartment to put it away. When she entered, Sally took the basket. "I'll put these away and keep an eye on the stove. You go see the foal," she said.

"Okay," agreed Lanie. She checked on the stove and went out the back door and down to the barn.

When Lanie entered the barn, she saw Marcel standing at the stall, gazing at the foal and talking to the mare. He turned when she came in and smiled at her. He came over and took her hand and led her over to the stall.

Lanie looked down at the foal butting its head into its mother's side and smiled. "She is beautiful," said Lanie.

"Yes, she is," agreed Marcel. He looked at Lanie. "I was going to ask if you wanted to come and see her earlier, but you were busy."

Lanie smiled up at him and squeezed his hand. "I was just doing a little cleaning. I'm here now."

"Yes, you are," agreed Marcel putting his arm around her and holding her close. Lanie snuggled into his embrace. It made her feel happy and loved.

They heard a car outside, and Logan came into the barn, followed by Hank. They grinned at Lanie and Marcel. "We had to come see the new addition," said Logan.

They both came over and gazed down at the new foal.

"Nice," said Logan.

"When are the others due?" asked Hank.

"Anytime," answered Marcel.

"You know we will have to bring everyone over to see the foal," said Logan.

"I know," agreed Marcel. "If they wait a couple of days, they might see more than one."

Logan shook his head. "They won't wait. They will just have to make repeat trips for the others."

Lanie laughed. "They already know about the foal. Chris told them this morning as soon as he got on the school bus."

"It's settled. We'll see you after the bus drops them off this afternoon," said Logan. Marcel smiled and accepted the inevitable.

They told Logan and Hank goodbye as they left. After spending a few more minutes gazing at the mare and foal, Marcel and Lanie started for the house.

After being warned about company coming, Lanie decided she had to have something to serve them. She looked around the pantry and refrigerator, thinking, what could she feed such a large bunch? Then she started smiling. She gathered things she needed and placed them on the counter. First, she made up dough and rolled it out. She took down a mixing bowl and chopped up peppers and onions, she added seasonings and then several different cheeses. She cut the dough into squares. In each square she placed a spoon of the cheese mixture. She folded the squares over and squeezed the sides until they were closed. When she had a pan of about three dozen squares, she popped them in the oven to brown. While they were cooking, she made another panful.

She kept an eye on the first pan so it would not get too brown. When it was ready, she set it out to cool while she put the next pan in to cook. While it was cooking, she made a couple of pitchers of tea. She took the second pan of poppers out of the oven to cool and put the tea in the fridge.

Lanie found two bowls and lined them with cloths. She rolled the poppers in powdered cheese and put them in the two bowls. She set them on the table to be served later. She found some paper cups and set them on the table. Rubbing her hands with satisfaction, Lanie hoped the people here liked her poppers as much as Chris did.

She started toward the living room and heard a knock on the door. Marcel was opening it and greeting Daisy and Doris.

"Hi," said Lanie, giving Daisy a hug. Where's Willow?" she asked.

Daisy laughed. "She said she had better wait and come over with Joey or she would have a very disappointed little boy on her hands."

"What smells so good?" asked Doris.

"I made some poppers," said Lanie. "Would you like to try them?"

"You bet," said Doris. "Ever since I found out I was expecting, I have been craving food."

"Congratulations," said Lanie. "Come with me. We can't deprive a pregnant lady," she teased.

They followed her to the dining room, and Doris's eyes lit up at the sight of the bowls full of poppers. She reached over and took one and popped it into her mouth. "Oh, this is so good," she said, savoring the flavors.

Lanie offered one to Daisy and Marcel, who had followed them to the dining room. They both ate them with enjoyment.

"There's only one thing wrong," said Marcel.

"What?" asked Lanie.

"You didn't make enough of them," he said.

"I made six dozen," said Lanie.

Daisy laughed as Doris reached for another popper and popped it into her mouth. "We'll just have to keep the men away from them," she said.

"I think we're too late," said Lanie as Marcel reached for another popper.

Marcel raised his hands. "I won't eat any more if you promise to make me some more later," he said, putting his arms around her and kissing her.

"No fair," teased Doris. "You have an unfair advantage. I want the recipe. Then I can make my own."

Lanie laughed. She loved the playful atmosphere of family teasing.

"Do you ladies want to go see the foal and leave some poppers for the rest?" asked Marcel.

"I suppose so," said Doris with a look at the poppers.

"I'll write the recipe down for you," promised Lanie. They all went out the back door and went down to the barn.

"Oh, how sweet," cooed Doris. Daisy laughed.

"She's adorable," agreed Daisy. "Babies are always so sweet, whether they are human or animal."

"Yes, they are," said Lanie. She remembered holding Chris in her arms. Marcel put an arm around her and held her close to his side. It was like he knew what she was thinking. Lanie laid her head against his shoulder.

"I need to go check on my stew," said Lanie. "I'll be back in a minute,"

Marcel hugged her and let her go. "Hurry back," he said.

Lanie smiled at him and left. She stirred the stew and added some more water. When satisfied it was alright, she quickly wrote down the recipe for the poppers and went back to the barn. Lanie gave the recipe to Doris, who looked at it and smiled.

"Bless you," she said. "Mark will bless you too, when he doesn't have to go and hunt up what I am craving in the middle of the night."

Daisy laughed. "You might think she's kidding, but Glen can tell you stories about some of the things he found for me in the middle of the night."

They all laughed again, but Lanie looked away. She had not had anyone to help her in the middle of the night when she had been expecting Chris.

Marcel hugged her close. "You will next time," he said softly."

Lanie looked up at him with misty eyes and smiled. "I know," she said.

They heard the bus stopping out front, and Lanie looked out the barn door to wave at Chris. He was headed for the house, but when he saw Lanie, he turned toward the barn. He gave Lanie a quick hug and handed her his backpack. As soon as his hands were free, he headed for the stall with the new foal.

Chris stood looking down at the foal with love on his face. He was quite entranced with the new addition to their ranch. He reached out a hand to touch the foal, but the mare made a quick movement to stand between her baby and the world.

Marcel rubbed the mare's head and talked to her.

"It's okay, lady. He just wants to meet your baby. He won't hurt her," said Marcel.

The mare shifted back, and Chris gently rubbed the foal's nose.

"See, everything is fine," Marcel soothed the mare.

Lanie smiled. She knew just how the mare felt. Marcel's voice could charm anyone. It sure worked with her.

Marcel looked over at her and grinned. Lanie smiled back at him. She could swear he was reading her mind.

Marcel just smiled and kept talking to the mare. Lanie turned to Chris. "We need to get you changed and get your homework done before anyone else comes," she said. She handed him his backpack to carry to the house.

"We need to go, too," said Daisy. "Too many of us at one time disturbs the mare. We will be back over when the other babies are here."

She and Doris followed Lanie and Chris out and back to the house. They went in the back door, and on the way to the front where Daisy was parked, Doris grabbed two more poppers.

"Oh, you made poppers," said Chris. "Cool."

"Wash your hands and change your clothes before eating," said Lanie. Chris gave one quick look of longing at the poppers and ran to obey.

Lanie gave Daisy and Doris a hug goodbye and thanked them for coming over.

"We enjoyed seeing the new baby," said Doris. "I loved the poppers. If you have any more ideas up your sleeve, be sure and let me know. I have a feeling the next seven and a half months are going to try everyone's patience."

Daisy shook her head and took Doris's arm to lead her outside. Lanie followed them out and waved goodbye to them as they drove away.

Lanie saw another car stopping. It was Willow and Logan. Lanie waved but went back inside to see about Chris. Marcel could handle the company.

Lanie sat Chris down at the table and gave him a glass of tea and three poppers. She gave him his homework to do while he was snacking.

Willow and Joey came in the back door. Willow was carrying Camille. Logan had stayed at the barn with Marcel.

Lanie sat Joey down at the table with Chris and gave him a glass of tea and three poppers. The boys talked while enjoying their snack.

Willow ate one, but she kept it away from Camille. "I don't think you are old enough for them," said Willow to Camille with a smile.

Sally came into the kitchen and took Camille from Willow. "Is it okay if I take her to our apartment to play for a while?" asked Sally.

"Sure," agreed Willow with a shrug.

Sally carried Camille to the apartment to play with some of Chris's stuffed toys. She was very happy sitting in the middle of the floor surrounded by a bunch of stuffed toys. Chris had a stuffed airplane she was fascinated by.

Lanie offered Willow a seat and a glass of tea. Willow took both, gratefully, and reached for another popper.

"Could I get the recipe for these?" asked Willow. "They taste great, and they make a great snack."

"Sure," agreed Lanie. "I have already given the recipe to Doris."

Willow laughed. "I bet they really hit the spot with Doris. I remember when I was pregnant; something like these poppers would have been great."

"I made up the recipe when I was carrying Chris," said Lanie.

"You made up the recipe!" exclaimed Willow.

"Yes, I did. As far as I know, no one else has ever made them," said Lanie.

"I need to take a sample of your poppers to Lizzy Wilde Eagle. She has a bakery in town. I think she would pay you well for a share of the recipe," said Willow.

"You really think so?" asked Lanie. "I never thought about selling the recipe."

"Wrap me a couple of the poppers in a napkin, and I will take them to Lizzy and see what she says," instructed Willow.

Lanie wrapped three of the poppers in a napkin and put them in a plastic bag and gave them to Willow. Willow put the bag in her purse.

"I'll let you know what she says as soon as I take them to her tomorrow," said Willow.

"Okay, thanks," said Lanie.

Willow looked over at Joey and Chris where they were sitting talking about Chris's homework. Joey was showing Chris some things he didn't know, and Chris was explaining some things Joey didn't understand.

"I need to round up Camille and take Joey home so he can do his homework," said Willow. "Joey, go tell your dad we are ready to go."

'Okay, Mom," said Joey as he ran out the back door.

Lanie led the way to her apartment. When they opened the door, she and Willow stopped and laughed at the sight of Camille in the middle of the floor with Sally. Both of them were just about covered in stuffed toys, and Camille laughed happily as she piled more toys over Sally and herself.

"I'd say she was having a good time," said Willow. "I know who to call if I need a babysitter."

"Anytime," laughed Sally in agreement.

"You ready to come with Mommy?" asked Willow.

Camille smiled at them and kept on playing.

Sally laughed and got up, raining stuffed toys. She reached down and lifted Camille and hugged her. She reached back down and picked out a small kitten. She gave it to Camille. Camille accepted it with a laugh and hugged it tightly.

"She can take it with her," said Sally. "Chris thinks he is too old for it."

Willow reached for Camille. Camille happily went to her mom. As long as she had her kitten, she was okay. They went back to the dining room to find Joey, Logan, and Marcel coming in the back door.

"Stanley is with the newborn," said Marcel when Lanie looked at him. He came over and kissed her cheek. He then reached over and popped a popper in his mouth.

Logan, seeing Marcel eating, reached in and popped one in his mouth. He chewed and immediately reached for another.

"These are good," he said.

"Yes, they are," agreed Willow.

Lanie reached for a tablet and wrote down the recipe and, tearing the page out, handed it to Willow.

"We have to get the kids home so Joey can do his homework," Willow told Logan.

Logan reached over and grabbed another popper before following her to the front door.

Lanie, Marcel, and Chris followed them out and stood on the porch while they got into their car to leave.

Everyone waved goodbye as they left, even Camille. Lanie, Marcel, and Chris waved back as long as they could see the car.

Lanie turned to Chris, "Inside," she said. "Finish your homework. And no more poppers for now. You will spoil your supper."

"Yes, Ma'am," said Chris as he went inside.

Lanie looked up at Marcel and smiled. Marcel pulled her close and kissed her.

"Ummmm, this is nice. I could get used to this," whispered Lanie.

"I certainly hope so," said Marcel as he kissed her again.

CHAPTER 10

The next day, after Willow saw Joey off on the school bus, she put Camille into her car seat and headed for Lizzy Wilde Eagle's bakery. It was located on the main business street on the reservation. It was in a convenient location to pick up a lot of business from the other stores and businesses in downtown.

Willow went in and smiled at Lizzy. She had gone to school with her, and they knew each other well. Lizzy was seated at a table with her uncle. Willow knew who he was, but she had not been introduced to him.

"Hi, Lizzy," said Willow, stopping at Lizzy's table.

"Hi, Willow, how is Camille doing?" asked Lizzy.

"She's growing like a weed and beginning to get into everything," responded Willow.

"Willow, this is my uncle, Clyde War Eagle, from New York. Uncle Clyde, this is my friend Willow Black Feather," said Lizzy.

"It's nice to meet you," said Clyde, rising and shaking her hand.

"My boys, Rock and Stone, were friends with the Black Feather boys before we moved to New York," said Clyde.

"Logan Black Feather is my husband," said Willow.

Clyde held a chair for her to sit with them and then reseated himself.

Willow smiled at Lizzy. "This may not be the best time for this, but the reason I came by today was to let you do a taste test on an appetizer I had yesterday." Willow took the plastic bag out of her purse and gave it to Lizzy. Lizzy took the bag and opened it. She unwrapped the poppers and looked them over.

"What is it?" asked Lizzy.

"It's a cheese popper. Marcel's mate, Lanie, served them yesterday. They are her recipe. I wanted to see what you thought about them," said Willow.

Lizzy took one of the poppers and bit into it. She chewed slowly and savored the taste. Lizzy smiled at Willow.

"It's good," she said.

She handed one to Clyde and told him to taste it. Clyde bit into his popper and smiled at Willow.

"You said Lanie served them yesterday. Do you where she got the recipe?" he asked.

"She made it up. As far as I know, no one else has the recipe," said Willow.

"What do you think, Uncle Clyde?" asked Lizzy.

"I think we have a hit. These are great. We need to talk to Lanie and see if she is willing to part with her recipe," said Clyde.

Willow smiled. "I am sure she will," said Willow.

"If we make a deal," said Lizzy, "it has to be stipulated I can make them to serve in my bakery."

Willow looked puzzled. "Where else would you serve them?" she asked.

Lizzy smiled. "My uncle owns The War Eagle Restaurant in New York," said Lizzy. "I worked there to train before I opened my bakery. I was missing the reservation, so Uncle Clyde helped me open my bakery."

"Oh," said Willow. "I didn't know."

Clyde smiled. "Here on the reservation, I am not a big restaurant owner. I am just a native visiting my hometown," he said. "Do you think you can arrange for us to talk to Lanie?"

"Sure," said Willow. "When do you want to meet?"

"As soon as possible, I will only be here a few days," said Clyde.

Willow took out her phone and called Lanie. "Hi, Lanie, are you busy?" asked Willow.

"No, I just finished cleaning the kitchen. What's up?" asked Lanie.

"I am talking to Lizzy and her Uncle Clyde. They loved your poppers and would like to talk to you about them. Can you come down to Lizzy's bakery?" she asked.

"Sure, let me tell Marcel and Sally. I'll see you in a little bit," said Lanie.

Lanie called Marcel on his cell phone. He was down at the barn. When she explained about Willow taking her poppers to Lizzy, he told her he would be right there. Lanie told Sally she was going out, and Sally decided to go along. She wanted to go shopping.

Marcel came through the front door. He had already brought his car to the front.

"You didn't have to take off and take me," said Lanie. "I could have driven myself."

"I wanted to go with you," said Marcel giving her a quick kiss. "Hello, Sally. Are you going with us?"

"Yes, if you don't mind. I thought I would do a little shopping," said Sally.

"I don't mind," said Marcel. "I am glad you are getting out and making friends."

It wasn't far, and they were soon going into Lizzy's bakery, after dropping Sally at the clothing store.

Willow waved at them from the table where she was sitting with Lizzy and Clyde.

Marcel guided Lanie over to the table. "Hi, Lizzy. Hi, Mr. War Eagle," said Marcel. "This is Lanie. Lanie, this is Lizzy Wilde Eagle and her uncle, Clyde War Eagle. I don't know if you remember me,

Sir, but I am Marcel Black Feather. My brothers and I are friends of Rock and Stone."

"I remember you," said Clyde. "I have very fond memories of all of the things my boys used to get up to with you Black Feather boys," he said with a smile as he rose to shake their hands and offer Lanie a seat.

Marcel laughed as he pulled up another chair. "How are Rock and Stone doing? The only news I have of them these days is from Lizzy," said Marcel.

"They are both doing fine," said Clyde. "Both are married and working in my restaurant. They have presented me with five grandchildren. We are going to have to invite you all to New York for a visit sometime. I'm sure they would love to see all of you and catch up."

"It would be great to see them," said Marcel. "You wanted to talk to Lanie about her poppers?"

Clyde smiled at Lanie. "Willow said you made up the recipe for the poppers. Are you willing to talk about selling the recipe?" he asked.

"I guess so; I never thought about it. They were just something I made up as a treat for my son," she said.

"We would have to apply for a patent and do a search to be sure there is not already a patent on the recipe," said Clyde. "If it comes back clear, we would be willing to pay you for the recipe and also give you two percent of all future profits. We would have complete control of the recipe, and it could only be used at our restaurant and Lizzy's bakery."

"Does that mean I couldn't make them anymore?" asked Lanie with a frown.

"No," said Clyde with a smile. "You could still make them for your family. You just could not sell them to anyone."

"Oh," Lanie looked at Marcel. "What do you think?" she asked.

"I think we need to take this discussion to Dad's office. He could advise us and draw up the contracts if you decide to go ahead."

Lanie squeezed his hand. "If we decide to go ahead," she said.

Marcel smiled at her. "If we decide," he agreed. "Is it okay with you if we take this talk down the street to Dad's office?" he asked Clyde.

"Fine by me," said Clyde.

Marcel took out his phone. "I had better see if Dad is there and can see us," he said.

"Hello, April, is Dad in, and can he see us?" he asked.

"Yes, he is here, and I'm sure he can squeeze you in," she said.

"We're at Lizzy's bakery. We'll be there in a few minutes," said Marcel.

"Okay, I'll let him know to expect you," said April.

"He's expecting us. It's just a short walk. Are we ready to go?" asked Marcel, rising and helping Lanie up. He then turned to help Willow.

"I think I'm going to head home with Camille," said Willow.

Lanie turned and hugged her. "Thanks for helping. No matter what happens, I appreciate you trying," said Lanie.

"We are family. We will always be here for you," said Willow, giving Lanie a hug and leaving.

The others left the bakery and walked the short distance to Glen Black Feather's office.

He was waiting for them when they arrived. April had informed him of their coming.

Glen came forward and gave Lanie a hug. He shook Lizzy's hand and turned to Clyde.

"Clyde," he said, smiling big and holding out his hand. "It's good to see you. How are you and your family doing in New York?"

"We are doing great," said Clyde, shaking Glen's hand. "It's good to catch up with old friends."

"Yes, it is," agreed Glen. "What did you all want to talk about?"

"They are interested in the recipe for my cheese poppers," said Lanie.

Glen started grinning. "I heard about them last night. Daisy was talking about how good they were, and Doris made Mark go to the store for ingredients so she could make some."

"We would like to buy exclusive use of the recipe, after a patent search, if it's clear," said Clyde.

"Are you okay with selling your recipe, Lanie?" asked Glen.

Lanie gripped Marcel's hand and looked at him. Marcel smiled and nodded. "I'm fine with it, as long as you are in charge of the paperwork. I know you will keep everything straight," said Lanie.

"What are you offering?" asked Glen.

"We will pay five thousand dollars for the original recipe and two percent of the future profits," said Clyde.

Glen looked at Clyde and smiled. "Lanie will take seven thousand five hundred dollars and three percent of future profits," said Glen.

Clyde grinned. "Okay," he agreed.

"April, have the papers drawn up for everyone to sign," said Glen.

April turned and went to have the secretary fill in the proper papers for everyone to sign.

"So," said Glen while they were waiting. "How long are you going to be here?" he asked Clyde.

"I am just going to be here a few days. I flew in to check on my mom. She won't move to New York with us. She said the reservation is her home, and she's not moving until the Great Spirit comes for her," said Clyde.

Glen laughed. "A lot of the older folks feel like that. I wish we could instill some of the loyalty in our young folks. They all seem to want to spread their wings and fly away from the reservation."

"I'm sure some of them will return when they have had a taste of the world," said Clyde.

"Yes," agreed Glen. "Some do return. It is sometimes hard for them to come back after being away. They don't seem to know where they fit in. We are trying to help all we can. Moon Walking is a big help."

"Ah, Moon Walking," said Clyde with a smile. "How is she?"

"She is fine," said Glen. "I don't know how we would manage without her."

April brought the papers back into the room. She gave Glen one set. She gave Lanie a set and handed a set to Clyde and Lizzy.

"Could I have a copy, too?" asked Lizzy.

"Sure," said April. "I'll be right back." She quickly brought Lizzy a copy of the contract.

Lanie and Marcel had been reading her copy. "It says just what was agreed on," said Lanie.

"It says on here your name is Delaney Melton," said Clyde.

"Yes, it is, everyone calls me Lanie though," said Lanie. "Why?"

"I was wondering if you would have any objection to having the cheese poppers named after you?" asked Clyde.

Lanie looked at him, startled. "I don't know," she said. "What would you call them?"

"I was thinking about calling them 'Cheese Poppers by Delaney,'" said Clyde.

"Are you okay with it, Lanie?" asked Glen.

Lanie looked at Marcel. He smiled. "I'm okay with whatever you want," he said.

"It would be kind of neat having my poppers named after me," said Lanie.

Glen looked at Clyde. "Make the upfront settlement an even ten thousand dollars and you can use Delaney's name," he said.

Clyde shook his head. "You drive a hard bargain," he said to Glen. "Okay, ten thousand dollars it is," he agreed.

"April, take these papers and have them redone with the adjusted price and giving permission to call the poppers Cheese Poppers by Delaney."

Glen handed all the contracts to April, and she took them to the secretary to be redone.

The secretary quickly changed the contracts on her computer and printed out five new copies. April took the new contracts and passed them around. Everyone looked them over, and Glen nodded for Lanie to sign. She signed her copy while Clyde signed his. They exchanged papers and signed each other's. April took theirs and gave them to Glen and had each of them sign Glen's copy. Glen signed each of the other copies April took Lizzy's copy around, and everyone signed it.

April took all of the contracts into the outer office and notarized them. She brought them back and passed them out.

"I'll have a check sent to you as soon as the patent clears," said Clyde.

"Send it to Glen's office," said Lanie. "He's handling all of my affairs."

"Okay," said Clyde. "It's been a pleasure meeting you, Lanie."

"It's been my pleasure," said Lanie.

"Tell Rock and Stone, hello," said Marcel.

"I surely will," agreed Clyde. They all shook hands, and Clyde and Lizzy left.

"I hope you don't mind me telling them to send the check to you without asking," Lanie said to Glen.

"It's fine. I would have suggested it if I had thought about it. I would like to keep an eye on the accounts anyway," said Glen. "How about I take you two to lunch to celebrate?" asked Glen.

"Sorry, Dad, we will have to make it later. Stanley texted me. I have another mare in labor. We have to head for home. Thanks for helping," said Marcel. He hurried Lanie out to the car, where Sally was waiting for them.

"Did you get your shopping done?" Lanie asked Sally.

"Yes, I found a new dress to wear to bingo," said Sally. "Did you complete a deal on the poppers?"

"Yes, as soon as there is a patent search, Lizzy's uncle will start making and serving them in his restaurant in New York," said Lanie.

"Why are we in such a hurry to get home?" asked Sally.

"Another mare is in labor," said Marcel.

"Oh," said Sally. "How exciting!"

"Yes, it is," agreed Lanie.

When they arrived at home, Marcel parked by the barn. They walked over to where Stanley was talking to the mare to soothe her.

"I think I'll head on to the house and put my dress away," said Sally.

Marcel smiled at her and nodded. Sally turned and headed to the house. Lanie continued over to the stall with Marcel.

"I put the new foal and its mama in a stall on the other side of the barn," said Stanley. "I didn't want to have the new mama upset with so much going on around her new baby."

"Good idea," said Marcel.

Marcel went into the stall with the mare. He checked her out and rubbed her head and talked to her soothingly. When he came out of the stall, he noticed the mare was noticeably calmer than when he entered.

CHAPTER 11

*L*anie smiled at Marcel as he came out of the stall.

"Is she alright?" asked Lanie.

"She's doing fine. We just have to wait," said Marcel.

Marcel put an arm around Lanie's shoulder and pulled her close to his side. Lanie stood there close to him and watched as they waited for nature to take its course.

Stanley looked at Lanie and Marcel. "Marcel is a great help with the mares. He can talk to them, and they are so busy listening to him they calm down and don't panic," said Stanley.

Lanie laughed. "I can understand. Listening to his voice is very calming," she said.

Marcel gave her a squeeze and smiled at her.

"You can listen to my voice anytime you want to," he thought. Lanie looked at him sharply.

"Did I just hear you when you weren't talking?" she asked.

Marcel grinned delightedly. "Yes, you did. Isn't it great?"

"Well, it will take a little getting used to, but it could come in handy," thought Lanie.

Stanley looked at Marcel and Lanie. They were just standing

there grinning at each other. Love sure was funny. It made sane people act weird, thought Stanley. He couldn't complain. The Black Feather family was great to work for. He loved being around the horses, and they all treated him like family. He was very lucky.

Marcel looked at Stanley. "We have a while before she delivers. I am going to walk Lanie up to the house. If you need me, call."

"Sure, Boss," said Stanley. "Milo wants to take off early. He promised to take Sally to bingo."

"Okay," said Marcel.

He took Lanie's hand in his as they left and started for the house. When they reached the front porch, Marcel led her to the swing and sat down and tugged her hand to get her to sit in his lap.

Lanie happily settled in his lap and leaned back against his shoulder and looked up at him. Marcel lowered his mouth to hers and kissed her. As Lanie pressed closer, Marcel deepened the kiss. When Marcel drew back, they were both breathing heavily. Lanie laid her face against Marcel to catch her breath.

"I love kissing," she said. "Do we have to stop? Breathing is overrated."

Marcel laughed and spread small kisses around her face. "We can work around it. I prefer you breathing," he said.

"Yeah, I guess so," agreed Lanie with a sigh. They settled back, and Marcel held her close and started the swing moving slightly.

"How could I hear you without talking?" asked Lanie.

"It's called mind talking. When two people are true loves, they can sometimes hear each other's thoughts if they try," explained Marcel.

"So, we are true loves?" asked Lanie, smiling into Marcel's eyes.

"Yes, I knew you were my true love the first time we met. It just took a while for you to admit," teased Marcel.

"I knew. I just couldn't admit it to myself," said Lanie. "I couldn't believe anything so wonderful could be happening to me."

"Believe it," said Marcel. "You are mine, and I'm never going to let you doubt it."

Lanie leaned up and pressed her lips to his. She drew back when she heard a car coming. Lanie looked toward the drive but made no move to get up from Marcel's lap. She leaned back against him comfortably.

Marcel was surprised to see Mark drive up with Doris. Orin and Sarah were with them. Mark open Doris's door and helped her out while Orin and Sarah scrambled out and ran toward the porch.

"Hi, Uncle Marcel," said Sarah. She smiled shyly at Lanie.

"Hi, Sarah, why aren't you guys in school?" asked Marcel.

"We had dentist appointments today, so we stayed home," said Orin.

"They stayed out of school. They didn't stay home," corrected Doris with a laugh. "Mark had the day off, so we decided to bring them to see the new foal."

Mark was walking with Doris, with his arm around her. "He looks very happy to be with his lady," thought Marcel. "I know how he feels."

Lanie smiled at Marcel. She had read his thoughts.

"I hope you don't mind us dropping by," said Mark.

"It's fine," said Lanie. "You are welcome anytime."

"We can go and see the foal, but we will have to be quick and quiet. Another mare is in labor, and I don't want to upset her," said Marcel.

"We can wait until tomorrow," said Doris.

"No, they can see the first foal," said Marcel. "They can be quiet. Can't you?" he asked. Both Orin and Sarah nodded solemnly.

Marcel laughed and helped Lanie up, so he could get up and take their visitors to the barn. He held Lanie's hand and led her along with them. Mark and Doris brought up the rear.

When they went in the door, Stanley glanced over at them and shook his head at Marcel's questioning look. Marcel turned in the opposite direction and led them to the mare and her foal.

"Ohhh," said Sarah as she gazed at the baby.

Orin gazed at it with wide-eyed awe. Mark and Doris watched them with indulgence.

"She is beautiful," whispered Sarah. "Have you named her?"

"Not yet," said Marcel. "Any suggestions?"

Sarah thought about it for a minute. "What is her mother's name?" asked Sarah.

"Her name is Agrego. It means Star Shine," said Marcel.

"What would Star Light be?" asked Sarah.

"It would be Agrilo," said Marcel.

"Agrilo," said Sarah, trying out the name. She looked at Marcel to see what he thought about the name.

Marcel smiled. "I like it. Hey there, little Agrilo. How do you like your new name?"

Agrilo sniffed Marcel's hand. He was holding it down to her. "I guess she approves," said Marcel.

"We need to go out," said Mark. "Before we bother the new mother-to-be." They all turned, and with one last look at Agrilo, they left the barn.

When they were outside, the two youngsters asked if they could go to play in the treehouse. Marcel nodded, and they ran toward the tree. Marcel, Lanie, Doris, and Mark made their way to the porch and relaxed in the swings. Both guys pulled their ladies close to their sides.

"Do you know if you are having a boy or girl?" asked Lanie.

"Not yet; I'll find out at my next appointment," said Doris.

"It doesn't matter," said Mark. "It will be loved either way."

Doris gave him a misty smile, and he hugged her closer.

"You certainly have a beautiful house," said Lanie, changing the subject.

Doris laughed. "It was all Mark. He was determined the house was going to be just right for us. He kept a close eye on the builders. They were afraid to do anything without checking with him first."

Mark grinned. "It worked, didn't it? They built the house the way it was supposed to be and no shortcuts," he declared.

"They did," agreed Doris, "and I love it." She gave his arm a squeeze.

"Did Gunner decide about the job?" asked Marcel.

"He is still thinking about it. I think he will stay. May and Silas offered him and Brenda a fifteen-acre lot to build a house on if they stay. It is on the corner of their land closest to Rolling Fork. "He wouldn't have far to drive to go to work. And Brenda would be close enough to visit with May," said Mark.

Marcel grinned. "It sounds like May and Silas want them to stay enough to sweeten the deal."

"May and Gunner are very close, and Brenda is her best friend," said Doris.

While they were sitting there talking, the school bus drove up, and Chris got off. He waved at Joey as the bus left. Then he ran to the porch and greeted Lanie and Marcel.

Chris looked at Doris and Mark and said hello.

"Hello, Chris," said Doris. "Orin and Sarah are in the treehouse."

"Can I go play, Mom?" asked Chris.

"Yes, go ahead," said Lanie.

Chris was running towards the treehouse before she finished talking. Lanie smiled at Marcel and shook her head. Marcel squeezed her hand.

Marcel's phone beeped with a text message. He looked at it and then started rising.

"Stanley said the foal is getting ready to be delivered," said Marcel. He helped Lanie up while Mark helped Doris, and they all headed for the barn.

When they entered the barn, they found Stanley talking to the mare trying to calm her. It wasn't working. She was very agitated.

"We need your soothing voice, Boss. They don't like mine," said Stanley.

Marcel moved from Lanie's side and went to the mare's head. He started talking to her in a soft voice and rubbing her around her head.

The mare calmed down and listened to Marcel. She was much calmer.

"What did I tell you?" asked Stanley. "They love the sound of his voice. He is a horse whisperer." Marcel didn't pay him any attention. He focused on the mare.

"I've seen him do it for years," said Mark. "I have no idea how he does it, but it works."

"He does it with love," said Lanie. "He loves them, and they feel it, so they listen."

Mark looked at her in surprise. "You may be right. I never thought of it like that, but it makes sense."

"Yes, it does," agreed Doris. "I know when you talk like that to me, I get all mushy inside and calm right down," said Doris to Mark.

"I'll have to remember to sweet talk you if we disagree," said Mark.

"Just remember it works both ways," replied Doris.

"I'll look forward to it," grinned Mark, hugging her.

Stanley gave a grunt, and they watched a colt slide into the world.

Stanley and Marcel helped him clear his breathing passages and let his mama clean him up. They all watched as the mare cleaned him and pushed him to stand and start nursing. Marcel and Stanley went over to the large sink and washed up, all the while keeping an eye on mother and son.

Doris turned misty-eyed and hid her face in Mark's chest. He held her close. "It is so beautiful, watching a new life begin," said Doris.

"Yes, it is," agreed Lanie.

Mark came over and put an arm around her and held her close as they watched the new colt latch on and start nursing.

"He's going to be fine," said Marcel.

Chris stuck his head in the barn, looking for Lanie and Marcel. When he saw everyone watching the new colt, he turned and motioned for Orin and Sarah to come. When they joined him, the three of them quietly walked over to where the adults were watching the new colt.

All three children smiled big when they saw the new addition.

"He's darling," said Sarah.

Orin looked offended. "He's a guy. He's tough. He is not darling," said Orin. All the adults smiled at this taste of male superiority.

"Well," said Lanie. "You and Chris are guys, and I think you both are darling."

"Mom," protested Chris. Orin flushed but did not say anything. He knew not to be rude to an adult.

Doris laughed. "I'm with you, Lanie. This male toughness has its place, but it should be kept in its place. Don't let it get out of hand." She warned Orin.

"Yes, Ma'am," said Orin.

"We need to get home. You guys have homework, even though you didn't go to school today," said Doris.

"I'm glad we were here for the main event," said Mark. "Thanks for enlivening my day off."

"Anything to help out," said Marcel teasingly.

They all headed for the front and Mark's car. After Mark helped Doris into her seat, he turned to see Orin and Sarah already buckled in their seats.

He shook Marcel's hand and kissed Lanie on the cheek and went to the driver's seat to leave.

After waving the car out of sight, Lanie, Marcel, and Chris headed inside.

"Get your clothes changed, and I'll make you a snack to eat before you do your homework," said Lanie to Chris.

CHAPTER 12

*W*hen Sally came out in her new dress, Lanie looked at her and smiled. Marcel whistled, and Chris looked up in surprise to see what the fuss was about.

"You look great, Sally," said Lanie.

"Thanks," said Sally, flushing slightly. "You don't think I'm making too much fuss for bingo, do you?"

"I think you will make just the right impression. You want to look your best so you will feel confident enough to relax and have a good time," said Lanie.

"You don't have anything to worry about, Sally. Milo will take care of you. My mom will be there, and Dad might go if Mom can talk him into it. They will make sure you make a lot of new friends. We all want you to be happy here," said Marcel.

Sally flushed and smiled happily. "I am happy here. I can't remember when I have been so happy. I don't have to worry about paying rent or wondering where my next meal is coming from. I am surrounded by people I care about and who care about me. I am blessed," said Sally, misty-eyed.

Lanie went over and gave Sally a hug.

"Have fun at bingo tonight, Nana," said Chris. "I hope you win." Everyone laughed, and the atmosphere was lightened.

There was a knock at the door, and Marcel went to show Milo in. Milo smiled at Sally. "You look great, Miss Sally," said Milo.

Sally smiled. "Thank you, Milo."

"You take good care of Sally tonight, Milo," said Marcel as he opened the door for them to go.

"I surely will, Mr. Marcel," said Milo as he smiled at Sally and took her hand to help her down the steps to his car.

Marcel waved them off and went back inside to find Lanie helping Chris with a question on his homework.

Marcel went over and kissed Lanie lightly. "I'm going to check on our new moms. I'll be back shortly," he said.

"Okay," said Lanie.

Chris grinned up at him. He was pleased to see his mom and Marcel together. It made him feel like he had a real family.

Marcel ruffled his hair as he left. Chris was even happy about that. He knew Marcel only did it because he liked him. Chris went back to concentrating on his homework. He wanted his mom and Marcel to be proud of his grades.

Chris finished a page and started a new page. "Mom, are you and Marcel going to get married?" he asked.

"Maybe," said Lanie thoughtfully. "Would it be okay with you?"

Chris smiled. "Yes, would he be my dad?" asked Chris.

"Yes, if Marcel and I are married, he would be your dad," said Lanie.

"I'd like Marcel to be my dad," said Chris.

"I'm glad," said Lanie.

She went about her preparations for supper, and Chris went back to his homework. They were both satisfied with the way things were going for their family.

≈

Sally and Milo arrived at the community center, and Milo escorted her inside. They were greeted by Daisy and Glen, who were seated at a nearby table and waved for them to join their group.

Milo seated Sally and went to get bingo cards for him and Sally before coming back and taking the chair beside her.

Sally smiled at Milo and thanked him for the cards. "You didn't have to get me cards. I could have gotten my own," she said.

"Its fine," said Milo. "I only got two for each of us. I don't know if you wanted more."

Sally shook her head and smiled at Milo. "Two is fine. I don't like to feel rushed when the numbers are called. I want to relax and enjoy myself," said Sally.

"I know what you mean," said Daisy. "I like to visit while I'm here. I don't want to worry about a table full of cards."

"Besides," said Glen. "She likes to keep an eye on my cards. She is always convinced I'm going to miss a bingo."

Daisy laughed. "He starts talking to a friend and he doesn't pay any attention to the caller," she said with a smile for Glen.

Glen leaned over and kissed her. "Why should I pay attention? I have you here to do it for me."

Milo looked at Sally. She had been smiling at the teasing going on between Daisy and Glen.

"Would you like something to drink?" asked Milo.

Sally shook her head. "Every time I get drinks at bingo, I end up spilling them. I have learned to wait until it's over to get drinks," said Sally with a laugh.

Milo smiled. We can stop at the drive-through and get something after bingo," he offered.

"I'd like that," agreed Sally.

Milo smiled with satisfaction. He was really glad Mrs. Black Feather had suggested him for bringing Sally to bingo.

The bingo caller called for attention, so they all turned their attention to listening for numbers.

The third game in, Daisy had a bingo. Even though she had to split the bingo with three other people and only won ten dollars, you would think she had won big, she was so excited. Sally smiled as she watched her new friend accept a kiss from her husband and wave her money around. The other people at the table were smiling, too. To see Daisy so happy made them all happy. Daisy was a well-loved person on the reservation.

When the games were over, Milo and Sally said goodbye to the others at their table and made their way outside. Daisy and Glen followed them out and Daisy gave Sally a hug and told her she would be watching for her next Thursday.

"I had a good time," said Sally. "I'm really glad I came."

They all left, and Milo drove through the local drive-through for their drinks. Some of the others must have had the same idea because they recognized several people from bingo, and they all waved at Milo and Sally. Sally and Milo waved back happily as they inched their way forward to be served.

They had been talking quietly. Milo was asking questions about Sally's life in Liberty, and Sally asking Milo about working for the Black Feather family.

They finally reached the window and ordered their drinks. They started drinking them on the way home.

When they arrived home, they sat in the car and finished their drinks before getting out. When they finished the drinks, Milo walked Sally to the porch. Sally turned and smiled at Milo.

"Thank you for taking me to bingo, Milo. I had a great time," said Sally.

"Thank you for going with me, Miss Sally. I had a great time, too," said Milo.

Milo reached for her hand and squeezed it gently.

"I was wondering, Miss Sally," said Milo.

"What were you wondering, Milo?" Sally asked with a small smile of encouragement.

"I was wondering if you would like to go to a movie with me sometime?" asked Milo shyly.

"Do we have a movie theater on the reservation?" asked Sally.

"No, we would have to drive into Rolling Fork," said Milo.

"Oh," said Sally. She grinned at Milo and squeezed his hand she was still holding. "I would love to go to a movie with you, Milo."

Milo smiled big and squeezed her hand again. "Thanks," he said. "I'll find out when they have a good movie showing and let you know."

"Okay," said Sally. "I'll be waiting to hear from you. Good night, Milo. I'll see you tomorrow."

"Good night, Miss Sally," said Milo. He watched as Sally turned and headed for the door. She turned as she entered and looked back. With a smile and a little wave, she went in and closed the door.

Milo smiled and went to take his car to the garage to put it away.

Sally smiled at Lanie and Marcel, who were curled up together on the sofa.

"Did you have a good time?" asked Lanie.

"Yes, I did." She looked at Marcel. "Daisy won at bingo. It was only ten dollars, but she was pleased."

"I bet she was," said Marcel. "She loves winning. It's not the amount; it's the excitement of winning. She'll take the ten dollars and buy food to give to a poor family. She never keeps her winnings. She told us one time, when we asked her why she didn't keep her winnings, if she kept the winnings when so many needed it more, the Great Spirit would not bless her with more winnings. She said, the Great Spirit knew she doesn't need the money, but as long as she helped the ones needing it, the Great Spirit would keep providing."

"That is beautiful," said Lanie. She looked at Sally, who was nodding.

Lanie looked back at Marcel. "I love your mom," said Lanie.

Marcel smiled and held her close. "So do I. I love you, too," he said and kissed her.

Sally cleared her throat, but she was smiling. Lanie and Marcel looked at her. "I'll say good night," she said as she headed for their apartment.

"Good night, Sally," said Lanie and Marcel.

Lanie settled closer into Marcel's arms and raised her face for another kiss. He was happy to oblige.

When they come up for air, Lanie looked at Marcel seriously. "What is it?" asked Marcel

"Chris asked me earlier if we were going to be married," said Lanie.

"What did you tell him?" asked Marcel.

"I told him maybe," said Lanie. "I wanted to see how he felt about it."

"How did he take it?" asked Marcel.

"He was fine with it. He wanted to know if you would be his dad," said Lanie.

"I would love to be his dad if it is okay with you and him," said Marcel.

Lanie placed her hands on his face. "After marrying you, having you be Chris's dad would be my dream come true," said Lanie.

"Are you saying, you are okay with me adopting Chris and giving him my name?" asked Marcel.

"I'll ask Chris about it first, but I think he will love it. Since I am going to be a Black Feather, it is only right for my son to be one, too," said Lanie.

"You do realize you just agreed to marry me, don't you?" asked Marcel, grinning at her.

Lanie pretended to frown. "If you don't want to marry me," she started.

"No, you don't," said Marcel, pulling her close. "I'm not letting you back out now."

Marcel started kissing her like he would never stop. It was fine with her. She didn't want to stop. This was where she was meant to be, in Marcel's arms.

Marcel finally pulled back with a sigh. Lanie looked up at him. "I have to make a final check on the new foals before I turn in," said Marcel.

Lanie started to get up. Marcel held her for a minute.

"We are going to talk more about when we are getting married," he said. "It can't happen too soon for me."

Lanie smiled and kissed him. "Go check the babies. I am not going anywhere," she said.

Marcel went toward the back door, and Lanie lay back on the sofa and stretched.

She smiled as she thought about how everything had changed for her and Chris. They had gone from struggling to happy. She owed it all to the wonderful man who had just left her arms.

Marcel started across the yard toward the barn. He noticed a light on in the bunkhouse. He smiled. Milo must be getting ready to turn in.

Marcel went in the barn and turned on one light so it would not disturb the horses. He checked on one, then the other. They both were sleeping soundly. Marcel turned out the light and closed the door, making sure it was shut tight before heading for the house.

He went in the back door and washed his hands before going in search of Lanie. He found her sound asleep, stretched out on the sofa.

Marcel smiled. He picked up Lanie, holding her close in his arms. She snuggled closer but did not wake up. Marcel took her to her room and laid her on her bed. He removed her shoes and pulled the cover over her. Marcel leaned forward and kissed her gently.

"Ummmm," said Laney before settling back to sleep.

Marcel smiled and left her to go to his own lonely bed. It would not be long, he promised himself.

CHAPTER 13

$\mathcal{T}$he next morning, Lanie was cleaning the kitchen after seeing Chris off on the school bus. Marcel called her name as he came in the front door.

Lanie went to see what he wanted. It was strange for him to come in the front door after going to the barn to check on the mares and new babies. He usually came in the back door.

Lanie looked up in surprise when she entered the front room.

"We have company," said Marcel with a smile.

"Bobby Joe, Billy Joe, what are you doing here?" asked Lanie as she came forward to greet the brothers.

"We overheard some people talking to George in the bar, and we were worried about you," said Bobby Joe.

"Yeah," agreed Billy Joe. "We wanted to be sure you were alright and to warn you about what is going on."

"You drove all the way here just to warn me," said Lanie with a smile.

"You are our friend, and Ben asked to look out for you," said Bobby Joe.

"When did Ben ask you to look out for me?" asked Lanie.

"The day he was leaving. I guess he didn't know it was going to be forever," said Bobby Joe.

"Well, I appreciate your trying, but you don't have to worry anymore. I'm going to marry Marcel. He will look out for me," said Lanie.

They both smiled at Lanie and Marcel. "Congratulations," said both Bobby Joe and Billy Joe.

"Thank you," said Marcel. "What was the warning you wanted to deliver?"

"These two guys were in the bar. They were asking George questions about Lanie. They wanted to know what hours she worked and who took care of her son. They wanted to know if she dated anyone and if she drank or smoked. They asked other questions, but I don't remember all of them," said Bobby Joe.

"You did fine. You remembered a lot. Thanks, Bobby Joe," said Lanie.

Lanie looked at Marcel. "Why would anyone want to know all about me?" she asked. Marcel looked at her, and a light went off.

"The Meltons," they both said.

"We have more," said Billy Joe.

Lanie looked at him.

"After George got busy and moved out of earshot, the two guys were talking to each other. They didn't pay any mind to us, and we pretended to not be listening," said Billy Joe.

"What did they say?" asked Lanie.

"They were talking about waiting until some judge went on vacation and then taking their request before a woman judge. They seemed to think the woman judge was more favorable to grandparents. The reason we drove here was because they were talking about snatching the boy. They said the grandparents would have a better chance if they had physical custody," said Billy Joe. "We realized they were talking about Chris, and we wanted to warn you."

Lanie gasped and looked at Marcel. Marcel took out his phone and called reservation security.

"Hello, could I speak with Roy Hawk, please. This is Marcel Black Feather.

"Hello, Marcel, how can I help you?" asked Roy Hawk.

"Hello, Roy, I just received information about the Meltons, Lanie's former in-laws. It seems they are planning to try and kidnap Chris, Lanie's son, and try to gain custody of him away from her. We need some security at the school," said Marcel.

"I'll send Don and Tim over there. I heard you found your true love, congratulations," said Roy.

"Yes, I did," said Marcel, grinning at Lanie. "Thanks, Roy."

"He is sending Don and Tim over to the school," said Marcel while dialing another number.

"Hello, Principal Leopard, this is Marcel Black Feather," said Marcel

"Hello, Marcel, is something wrong?" asked Principal Leopard.

"Yes, Sir, I have been told someone is going to try and take Chris Melton. I have called Roy Hawk, and he is sending Don and Tim over to watch, but I wanted to alert you also. If you could keep an eye out and speak to the children. Tell them to not be alone. They need to stay in groups and never go over to talk to anyone they don't know. If someone tries to lure them away, they need to run to the teacher and get as far away from the person as they can."

"I'll call an assembly and talk to the students at once. I'll make sure Chris is protected," said Principal Leopard. "Thanks for alerting us to the problem."

Marcel hung up and looked at Lanie. "He will be fine. I'll have Stanley follow the bus home after school. Starting tomorrow, until everything is settled, I'll have a guard ride the bus to and from school," said Marcel.

Lanie smiled. "Thanks," she said, standing close to Marcel's side with his arm around her.

Marcel took his phone and called Glen. "Hi, April, could I speak with Dad?" asked Marcel.

"Hello, Marcel," said Glen.

"Hi, Dad, the Meltons have not given up. They are planning to try and kidnap Chris. It's alright. I have already alerted Roy and the school. They are also going to wait until Judge Hawthorn goes on vacation and try to push their custody attempt through a woman judge. She is supposed to favor grandparents' rights."

"Let me do some calling. I'll get back to you," said Glen.

"Thanks, Dad," said Marcel. "Dad will call back when he finds out what is going on."

"Boy," said Bobby Joe. "If I ever need help, I hope you are on my side."

Marcel smiled. "I am in your debt. If you need my help, just call."

"You don't owe us anything," said Bobby Joe. "Lanie is our friend. And, since she loves you, you are our friend, too."

Lanie smiled at the twins and then at Marcel.

"I told you they were good guys," she thought.

"Yes, they are," agreed Marcel.

Marcel stood up. "Let me go talk to Stanley and make sure he follows the bus home. Would you guys like to see our new foals?" asked Marcel.

"Yes," said Billy Joe. "I love seeing baby animals."

They all, Lanie included, went with Marcel out to the barn. Stanley was there, and Lanie and the twins stood gazing at the newborns while Marcel pulled Stanley aside and asked him to follow the bus home from school.

Meanwhile, Glen called Judge Hawthorn's office. He explained what the Meltons were up to and told him about the lady judge.

The Judge sighed. "I'm glad you called. I was about to take some time off. I know Judge Green has had a hard time since her son moved his family to Australia. We have tried to be understanding with her, but if she is making decisions enough to get talked about, her cases need to be investigated. We can't have her breaking up families. I may pretend to take off and see if we can flush the Meltons out. We need to settle this situation once and for all. I'll keep you updated. If you find out anything else, let me know," said Judge Hawthorne as he hung up.

He turned to the Governor. "It looks like our fishing trip may be delayed," he said. "Those Meltons are stubborn. How is the Attorney General's investigation coming along?"

The Governor shrugged. "They are working on the case. It seems they are having a bit of trouble getting all of the proof they need. All of the company funds have been hidden in offshore bank accounts. The Attorney General has some computer experts working on them. He is hoping to add tax fraud to the other charges against the company."

"What about the displaced families. What are they doing while the Attorney General plays 'find the money'?" asked the Judge.

The Governor smiled. "With the help of the Black Foundation, all of the families have been placed and are receiving assistance."

"Good," said the Judge.

"Well, are you ready to help me pretend to go on vacation?" asked the Judge.

"We can still go fishing," said the Governor. "We just have to keep our cell phones handy."

"Yes, we can," agreed the Judge. "I just need to alert my secretary to call me if the Meltons file for custody."

They left the office after the Judge talked to his secretary. They made sure everyone heard them talking about going fishing. When they reached the Governor's limo and driver, they were satisfied with their performance.

When Marcel, Lanie, and the twins came out of the barn, Bobby Joe turned to Lanie. "We need to start home. We have a long drive ahead of us," he said.

"Thanks for bringing us the news," said Lanie. "You guys take care of yourselves."

"We will," said Billy Joe. "We are going to find us a new place to hang out. We didn't like George telling them guys all about you."

"It might be better if you wait a while before changing," said Marcel. "You might overhear more information if people don't know you are interested."

"Okay," said Billy Joe. "We'll let you know if we hear anything else."

"Do you have my cell phone number?" asked Lanie.

The guys flushed slightly. "We have the number," said Bobby Joe. "We wanted to make sure you and Chris were okay."

Lanie and Marcel smiled.

"Now we see how happy you are, we won't worry anymore. If we hear anything, we will call," promised Billy Joe.

"Thanks, guys," said Lanie. She gave each of them a hug and waved to them as they got in their car and left.

Lanie went to Marcel and hugged him close. "Will we ever get rid of the Meltons?" asked Lanie.

"We will stop them. We have some powerful people working on taking them down. It just takes time," said Marcel.

Marcel gave her an extra squeeze and took out his phone again. "Hello, Jamie, are you and Silas busy?" asked Marcel.

"Not terribly," said Jamie. "What's up?"

"Lanie's former in-laws are threatening to try and kidnap her son, Chris. I need someone to ride the bus to and from school until we can stop them," said Marcel.

"Okay, we can do it. We can work around our hauling. If we can't make it sometime, maybe Don or Tim could help out," said Jamie.

"Roy sent Don and Tim to watch at school, but they could ride the bus sometime, too," said Marcel.

"Alright, I'll start in the morning. I'll catch the bus and ride the route," said Jamie.

"Thanks, Jamie," said Marcel. "I appreciate it."

"Sure thing," said Jamie. "I'm glad you are the last of you guys to find your mates."

"Why?" asked Marcel.

"There is always someone trying to stop true love's path," said Jamie.

"You are wrong," said Marcel.

"About what?" asked Jamie.

"I'm not the last. There is still Summer," said Marcel with a laugh.

"Great Spirit protect me, you are right. I had forgot about her," said Jamie. "We are in for it when she comes home."

"Let's not get ahead of ourselves," said Marcel. "Let's take care of one problem at a time."

"Okay," agreed Jamie. "I'll see you later.

They hung up, and Marcel turned back to Lanie. "Jamie and Silas are going to take turns riding the bus," said Marcel.

"I adore your family," said Lanie. "All you have to do is ask, and they are right there for you," said Lanie.

"Get used to it," said Marcel, pulling her close. "They are you and Chris's family now, too. Anytime you need them, they will be there for you."

"When is your sister, Summer, going to be finished with college?" asked Lanie.

"I think she has another year," said Marcel. "Why?"

"I heard you mention her, and I was curious," said Lanie.

"We have a while before we have to worry about her," said Marcel.

"Has Mom or Doris told you anything about the marriage bracelets?" asked Marcel

"No, do you exchange bracelets instead of rings?" asked Lanie.

Marcel led her over to the porch swing and sat down and pulled her into his lap.

"We can exchange both or either. It's entirely up to the couple," said Marcel.

"Where do you get the marriage bracelet?" asked Lanie.

"We make them. You make one for me, and I make one for you,

and we exchange them and have them blessed at the ceremony," said Marcel. "You don't wear them like a regular bracelet. They are worn above the elbow and are tied on. It is bad luck to remove them."

"Do you think we need any more bad luck?" asked Lanie with a frown.

"I consider finding you and Chris very good luck," said Marcel.

Lanie kissed him. "You are right," she said. "How do I make a marriage bracelet?"

"You could get Mom or Doris to show you how. I can't show you. We are not supposed to show them to our mates until we exchange them," said Marcel.

"If I mess it up, we can still exchange rings, can't we?" asked Lanie.

Marcel laughed and kissed her. "We can exchange rings, and if the bracelets do not work out, we can forget about them," said Marcel.

"Okay, I'll talk to Doris and Daisy and see what I can do," agreed Lanie.

"Good," said Marcel, kissing her again.

"I'll have to get Logan to give me some pointers. I haven't made one before either," said Marcel.

"Good," said Lanie. "I'm glad I'm not the only amateur."

Marcel kissed her again.

"You know, it's a miracle we get anything done," said Lanie. "All I want to do is stay in your arms and enjoy your kisses."

"I know. Me, too. I'm addicted. As soon as I leave, I find myself thinking up excuses to come and find you and hold you close," said Marcel. "I wonder if my brothers have this problem. If they do, I don't see how they leave and go to work."

"Maybe that's why they are all expecting or just delivered," said Lanie.

Marcel burst out laughing. "You are probably right," he said when he could quit laughing. "How do you feel about more children?" asked Marcel.

"How many more?" asked Lanie, looking up at him and frowning slightly.

Marcel shrugged. "I haven't thought about it. Maybe two or three," he said.

Lanie thought about it while she studied Marcel's face.

"We will see how it goes. It won't be so bad. I don't mind being pregnant, and I love holding the newborn baby. It will be so much better to have you there through the whole thing," said Lanie.

"I will be with you through everything," promised Marcel. "My face will be the first face our child sees when it is delivered."

Lanie looked at him with tears in her eyes. She blinked them away. "I love you," she said, leaning in and kissing him soundly. Marcel deepened the kiss.

When he pulled back and caught his breath, he smiled. "I love you, too. You and Chris are my life," he said.

CHAPTER 14

The next morning, Marcel and Lanie watched from the porch as Chris went to his school bus. Jamie waved from the door as he stepped out to let Chris on. Lanie and Marcel waved back and drew a breath of relief to know he was there. They had talked to Chris the night before, and after the principal had already talked to everyone at school, they were convinced Chris would be safe.

Marcel went to check on the horses, and Lanie had gone to clean the kitchen and straighten the bedrooms. After she finished cleaning, Lanie called Daisy to ask about the marriage bracelet. Daisy assured Lanie she would be able to make the bracelet and told her there were plenty of supplies at her house. Daisy promised to bring them over later in the day, so Lanie could look through and see if she could find what she liked to design a bracelet.

Daisy reminded Lanie to not work on it around Marcel. He was not allowed to see it until the ceremony.

"I promise to only work on it when he is out of the house," said Lanie.

Daisy laughed. "I know it seems silly, but it makes the bracelet more special when the design is a surprise," said Daisy.

"I understand," said Lanie. "Marcel knows he isn't allowed to see it. He won't cheat. We haven't set a date, yet, so we have a little more time to work on the bracelets. We have so much going on with the Meltons; we don't have time to prepare for a wedding."

"Don't let the Meltons run your life. Glen told me last night about the things they are pulling. He is hopeful we can get rid of their threat soon," said Daisy.

"I hope so," said Lanie. "I want to get on with my life and forget about them."

"We all hope Judge Hawthorn will be able to stop them and fix it so they will leave you and Chris alone," said Daisy.

"I hope so," said Lanie. "It's hard to believe they are trying so hard to take Chris from me when they haven't even tried to see him all these years," said Lanie.

"Hmmm, it is strange," agreed Daisy. "I'll see you later. I need to talk to Glen."

"Okay, thanks," said Lanie as she hung up the phone. She was very surprised at Daisy's abrupt ending of their conversation.

Daisy hung up the phone after talking with Lanie and then called Glen's office.

"Hello, Black Feather Law Office," said April.

"Hello, April, could I speak to my husband, please?"

"Sure, Mrs. Black Feather, just a minute."

"Hello, Daisy, is something wrong?" asked Glen.

"No, I am fine. I was just talking with Lanie, and she said something that made me think," said Daisy.

"What did she say?" asked Glen.

"She said she didn't understand why the Meltons were trying to take Chris after ignoring him all these years. I started thinking, maybe there is a reason they want Chris so bad," said Daisy.

Glen sat up, startled. "We have been so busy worrying about what they are doing, we completely ignored why they are doing it.

For anyone as mercenary as the Meltons, there would have to be a reason. Thanks, Love. Remind me to give you a big kiss when I get home," said Glen.

"I don't think you will need any reminders after all these years," said Daisy with a laugh.

"You are right. I love you. I will see you tonight," said Glen.

"I love you, too," said Daisy, hanging up the phone.

After hanging up the phone with Daisy, Glen called a detective he used to investigate cases for him. He gave him all of the information he had on the Meltons and told him he was in immediate need of information on the Meltons' motives. The detective said he would get right on the case.

Glen tried to put the Meltons out of his mind and concentrate on other cases, but they kept popping up in his thoughts. He shook his head. How could he have missed such an obvious clue?

It was two hours later when his detective called him back.

"What do you have for me?" asked Glen.

"It was easy," said Grant. "I didn't even have to leave my office. I called a friend of mine in the records department in Kansas City. She looked up Melton. Christopher Melton popped right up. It seems an uncle of Timothy Melton died and left his money to Ben Melton and his descendants. Since Ben has died, the whole estate goes to Christopher. Timothy and Gladys Melton had it recorded and listed themselves as Christopher's guardian. They have to have proof of guardianship before they can access the money. They only have a short time to bring the proof and show it to the records clerk."

"I see why they are in such a hurry to get their hands on Chris," said Glen. "What is the amount of the inheritance?"

"Eight million dollars," said Grant with a laugh.

"Wow, it's a wonder they didn't try to have Lanie killed so no one could stop them. For that kind of money, people will do anything," said Glen. "Can you get me some documentation to take to court?" asked Glen.

"It is already on its way. Your fax machine should be getting it any time now," said Grant.

"Thanks, Grant, I'll let you know if I need anything else," said Glen.

Glen hung up the phone and called Marcel.

"Hello, Dad," said Marcel.

"Marcel, where is Lanie?" asked Glen.

"She is up at the house," said Marcel. "Why?"

"It is not just Chris who is in danger. It's very possible the Meltons have taken a hit out on Lanie," said Glen.

"Why would they do that?" asked Marcel.

"So, they can have themselves named Chris's guardians," said Glen. "Chris has inherited eight million dollars from a distant uncle of his father's. The Meltons had it registered and named themselves Chris's guardians. They can be his guardians through court or by getting rid of Chris's mother."

"I see," said Marcel. "Will you call Roy and alert him? I need to go talk to Lanie."

"Okay," agreed Glen.

Marcel hung up the phone and took off at a run to the house. When he reached the porch, he stopped and looked out over the ranch. He shook his head. He couldn't see anything suspicious, but it was a big ranch, and there were many places someone could hide.

Marcel turned and went inside. "Lanie, where are you?" he thought.

"I'm in the kitchen," thought Lanie.

Marcel headed for the kitchen. As soon as he entered, he pulled Lanie into his arms and held her close.

"What's wrong?" asked Lanie, hugging him back.

"I just found out why the Meltons are so determined to get Chris," said Marcel. "Chris has an inheritance through a distant uncle of Ben's. The Meltons want control of the inheritance, and one of the ways they could get it is by having you eliminated so they would be Chris's guardians."

"How much is the inheritance?" asked Lanie.

"Eight million dollars," said Marcel.

"What!" exclaimed Lanie. "I'm surprised they haven't already tried to eliminate me."

"I think we moved too fast for them," said Marcel.

"Well, we just have to stay one step ahead of them," said Lanie, pulling back and going to her phone.

"April, this is Lanie. Could I speak to Glen, please?"

"Hello, Lanie. I guess Marcel gave you the news," said Glen.

"Yes, he did. I think I have a way to stop the Meltons in their tracks," said Lanie.

"What do you have in mind?" asked Glen.

"Could you arrange for a private marriage ceremony in your office this afternoon?" asked Lanie.

"Yes, I can call Derrick and get him over here," said Glen.

"Good," said Lanie. "I also want you to draw up adoption papers for Marcel to adopt Chris and draw up a will for me leaving custody of Chris to Marcel and then to the entire Black Feather family if anything happens to me."

"I'll have the papers drawn up and ready to sign by the time you and Marcel get here. I'll ask Moon Walking to call Derrick. He'll drop everything for her. Can you two be here in an hour?" asked Glen.

"Yes," said Lanie and hung up the phone.

Marcel had been listening to Lanie talk with his dad. He was frowning. Lanie looked at him.

"You do want to marry me, don't you?" she asked.

Marcel pulled her into his arms. "More than anything, I just don't want you to feel like you have to marry me. You know I would always take care of Chris. I already feel like he is my son," said Marcel

"I want to marry you. We were already planning to marry. This just speeds it up a bit. We can always have another ceremony later for the family. I want to be your wife in every way," said Lanie, kissing him.

Marcel kissed her back and grinned. "We had better get a move on," he said. "We have a wedding to attend." They both went to change before going to Glen's office and their future.

When Marcel and Lanie arrived at Glen's office, they found Daisy in the outer office talking to April. Daisy went over to Lanie and hugged her.

"Glen told me what was going on. When he told me you were getting married, I came right over," said Daisy.

"We are going to have another wedding later for everyone to attend," said Marcel.

Daisy hugged him, too. "I understand," said Daisy.

They all turned and looked as Derrick came in the door. He smiled and greeted everyone. "I have the marriage license here if we can get it filled out." Lanie and Marcel went over to the desk and answered his questions as Derrick filled out the paperwork. "I also brought the papers to allow Marcel to adopt your son. After I leave here, I will go by and have the board of Elders to sign the paperwork," said Derrick

They filled out and signed all of the papers. Daisy and April signed as witnesses, and the secretary notarized all of the papers.

Glen came out of his office. He had someone with him. "Grant, this is my wife Daisy, my son Marcel, my trainee April, our local Justice of the Peace, Derrick Bear, and Delaney Melton," said Glen. "Everyone, this is Grant Cross. He is the one who found out what the Meltons were up to."

"It's nice to meet you all," said Grant, smiling at them all.

Marcel went over and shook his hand. "Thanks for all of your help," said Marcel.

"Yes, thank you," agreed Lanie.

"If I can have everyone's attention," said Derrick. They all turned to stand in front of Derrick. He went through the ceremony quickly. When it came time for the rings, Derrick pulled a ring out of his pocket and handed it to Marcel.

"Moon Walking told me to give this to you," he said.

Marcel took the ring with a smile and repeating the words Derrick told him, he slid the ring on Lanie's finger. It was a perfect fit.

"You may kiss the bride," said Derrick.

Marcel obeyed, happily.

They thanked Derrick, and he left to take the adoption papers and get them approved by the Elders. After the Elders signed the adoption papers and notarized them, getting them signed in court was just a formality. Derrick also took a copy of Lanie's will to file in the records office in Rolling Fork. There was no better way to get the word out to the Meltons than to file it where the public had access to it. To be extra sure, Glen sent a notice to the Rolling Fork paper announcing Marcel and Lanie's marriage and Chris's adoption.

"We had better get home," said Lanie. "We need to tell Chris the news before he hears it somewhere else. I told Sally before we left, and she stayed behind so she would be there if we didn't make it back before the bus ran." They gave Daisy, Glen, and April hugs and accepted their congratulations before they left for home.

They arrived home before the bus, but Marcel would not let Lanie wait on the front porch. He wanted to be sure the Meltons had received the news before he chanced having Lanie out where she could be a target. Lanie didn't like it, but she understood.

Sally was amazed when she saw Lanie's ring and found out Moon Walking had sent it.

"I'm going to get you another ring," said Marcel. "You can wear this one as a dress ring."

"It is fine," said Lanie. "After all, we are going to have the bracelets for our next ceremony."

Marcel was happy Lanie still wanted to make and exchange a marriage bracelet. It meant a lot to the people on the reservation.

They heard the bus stopping, and Marcel went to the door. Jamie walked Chris to the door and waved the bus on. He stayed behind.

"April told me your news," he said. "Congratulations. She also told me what is going on. I thought I would hang around here for a while and keep an eye out for trouble."

"Thanks, I appreciate your help," said Marcel. "There are some rifles in my office. Help yourself."

"I'll check them out," said Jamie. "Silas is going to join me in a while."

"Okay," said Marcel. "I need to go inside. Lanie and I have to talk to Chris."

Chris had gone on inside, but Lanie waited for Marcel before she told him anything. She wanted them to tell him together. Marcel came inside and went over and kissed Lanie. Chris was sitting at the table, eating a snack. Sally was sitting with him, talking quietly. Lanie had been moving around nervously. She only hoped Chris was really okay with all she had done.

Chris looked at his mom, and Marcel and smiled. Marcel took Lanie's hand and drew her over to a chair close to Chris. "Chris, we want to talk to you," said Marcel. "You know when your mom asked you if you would be okay with me being your dad?"

Chris nodded his head.

"Well, I hope you meant it because your mom and I were married this afternoon, and I have applied to adopt you as my son," said Marcel.

Chris started smiling. "You really are going to be my dad?" said Chris.

"Yes, I am," said Marcel. Chris jumped up from his chair and threw his arms around Marcel. Marcel hugged him back. Chris drew back and looked at Marcel. "Is it alright if I call you Dad?" he asked.

"It is very alright. I would really like for you to call me Dad," said Marcel.

Chris hugged him once more and then turned to Lanie. He went to her and hugged her, also. "Thanks, Mom," he said.

"For what?" asked Lanie returning his hug.

"For giving me a dad," said Chris.

"It was my pleasure," said Lanie smiling at Marcel.

"We are going to have another wedding later, after this mess with the Meltons is resolved," said Lanie. "I found out why the Meltons are trying to take you," said Lanie.

"Why?" asked Chris.

"They found out about an inheritance you are getting. It was passed down to you through your father, Ben Melton. It was left by a distant uncle of Ben's. It was to be passed down to Ben's descendants. Well, you are his descendant. So, it was left to you, and the Meltons wanted you so they could control the money," said Lanie.

Chris thought a minute, then looked at Lanie and Marcel. "Couldn't we just give them the money so they would go away?" asked Chris.

"No, Chris, we can't give them the money. The money will be in a trust for you to use for college and for you when you are an adult. The Meltons would probably find ways around the trust, but we will make sure it stays there for your future," said Lanie.

"Oh," said Chris. "How are we going to stop them?" asked Chris.

"With the adoption, Marcel is now your dad. They have no claim on you. I also made out a will naming Marcel and the Black Feather family your guardians if anything happens to me," said Lanie.

Chris grinned. "So, I really am a member of the Black Feather family."

"Yes, you are. Your name will be Christopher Melton Black Feather," said Lanie.

"Wow," said Chris. "I know you said I was named after your dad, but now I will have my dad's name, too."

"Yes, you will," said Marcel, giving Chris another hug and smiling at him. They were all a little misty-eyed, even Sally.

CHAPTER 15

*I*t was about an hour later when everyone started arriving. Daisy and Glen came first with Glenda, Leon, and their baby. They were followed by Dawn, Hank, and their children. Logan, Willow, and their children were next. Mark and Doris came with Sarah and Orin. Mark had invited Gunner and Brenda to join them. Jamie and Silas had called for May and April to come over to join the group. Sally, Milo, and Stanley also joined the group. All of the women had brought food.

"We couldn't let the occasion go by without celebrating," said Daisy. "Even if you are going to have another wedding, our family just received two new members, and they have to be welcomed."

"Thank you," said Lanie. "Chris and I are honored to be a part of this wonderful family."

The party spilled over into the yard. The guys still kept an eye out for trouble, but they were not expecting any with such a large group there.

Some of the guys set up tables in the back yard, and some of the women, with the help of their husbands, strung streamers around. The other ladies were busy bringing out food.

Some of the children were playing in the treehouse. Others were just running around having a good time. Some of them were standing at the fence gazing at the horses. They were getting caught up in the family business early.

When the food was ready, Glen called everyone over to the tables. They all stood in a circle around the table and held hands. Chris stood between Lanie and Marcel, smiling at everyone.

"Great Spirit, we ask your blessing on the joining of Lanie and Marcel for their journey into a life together. We want to thank you for adding a new member to our family. We welcome Christopher Melton Black Feather to our family. Daisy and I are blessed to have a new grandson. We ask for you to watch over us all and continue to show us a light to follow," Glen ended his blessing with a smile at Chris.

"Wow," said Chris. "I have grandparents, too." Everyone laughed at his words.

"You certainly do, young Chris. We are here for you anytime you need us. Always remember, you are a Black Feather. It is a well-respected name on the reservation and in this country. Always be proud of your heritage."

"Enough," said Daisy. "I'm hungry. Let's eat." Everyone laughed and started filling plates.

Glen leaned over and kissed Daisy, drawing her close to his side. "Thanks for reminding when to stop talking," said Glen. Daisy just smiled and kissed him again, just because she wanted to.

They all had a great time stuffing their bellies and sitting around talking while the children ran around playing. Mark and Glenda's son and Logan and Willow's Camille were passed around and made a big fuss over.

It was getting late. The food had been cleared away, and the tables and chairs had been returned to the garage when groups started leaving. The children had school the next day, and the adults had work. There would be some tired people before the next day was over, but they all felt it was worth it.

Chris was fussed over by everyone and given a hug from Daisy and Glen. Milo and Stanley had slipped away earlier to check on the horses. Sally took Chris inside to get ready for bed. Lanie stood with Marcel's arms around her and enjoyed the night. They looked up at the stars and sighed together.

"We are finally alone, Mrs. Black Feather," said Marcel.

"Yes, we are, Mr. Black Feather," said Lanie turning in his arms and raising her lips for a kiss. Marcel started out kissing her gently, but he soon deepened the kiss and was kissing her passionately.

Marcel sighed as he drew back and laid his face close to hers. "We will continue after Chris is tucked in and sleeping," he said.

"Ummm, yes, we will," agreed Lanie. She smiled and headed inside, still holding Marcel's hand. She went to Chris's bedside to wish him good night.

Chris smiled up at them sleepily. "Good night, Mom. Good night, Dad," he said.

Marcel felt tears well up as he said good night and tucked Chris's blanket around him.

Lanie squeezed his hand and stayed close by his side as they wished Sally good night and went to their room.

Meanwhile, the Judge and the Governor were on a fishing trip, Governor style. They had a cabin, complete with internet and Wi-Fi. They had boats to go out on the lake to fish. The Judge went in one boat with one of the Governor's guards to handle the boat. The Governor was in another boat with another guard handling his boat. There were two more boats with security guards with them. The boats with the Governor and the Judge stayed close to each other so the two could talk. There were also guards scattered around on shore, keeping watch.

Whenever either of them caught a fish, they would take it to shore and give it to one of the guards to clean and hand over to the cook to prepare for eating later. They were both having a great time and catching a nice number of fish. When they decided to go in, they cleaned and packed away their fishing equipment so it would be ready for use later.

When they were inside, the Judge checked his messages. He was surprised to receive a long message forwarded from Glen through his secretary. Glen explained about the money and Lanie's solution to the problem. The Judge laughed and told the Governor about Lanie's solution.

"I like that girl," said the Governor. "She reminds me of Dora."

"I hope her plan works," said the Judge. "It would be nice for Marcel and Lanie to be able to get on with their lives without the shadow of the Meltons hanging over them."

The Governor's phone rang. He looked at the screen and saw the Attorney General was calling.

"Hello," said the Governor.

"Hello, Sir, I'm sorry for interrupting your vacation, but you wanted to know when we managed to get evidence on the group putting the families in Liberty out of their homes," said the Attorney General.

"Well," said the Governor. "Did you find the evidence?"

"Yes, Sir, my computer expert has unlocked their money transfers to offshore accounts and impounded the money. We have plenty of evidence to convict them of tax fraud in federal court. Warrants have already been issued for all of the members of the group."

"Good work," said the Governor. "We can discuss this more when I am back in my office."

The Governor hung up the phone and grinned at the Judge.

"There are federal warrants issued for the Meltons group for tax fraud. Their money has been impounded or frozen. I don't think they are going to be in any position to bother the Black Feathers for a long time," he said.

The Judge smiled. "Sometimes the good guys win," he said. "I'll send Glen a text in the morning before we go back out on the lake."

The old friends settled back to enjoy a nice visit with each other. The security guards were in their rooms or outside, so they had the illusion of being alone.

Moon Walking was gazing up at the night sky. She smiled at the beauty of nature.

"Sometimes Love's Gamble pays off," she said in a whisper.

THE END

Dear reader,

We hope you enjoyed reading *Love's Gamble*. Please take a moment to leave a review in Amazon, even if it's a short one. Your opinion is important to us.

Discover more books by Betty McLain at https://www.nextchapter. pub/authors/betty-mclain

Want to know when one of our books is free or discounted for Kindle? Join the newsletter at http://eepurl.com/bqqB3H

Best regards,

Betty McLain and the Next Chapter Team

The story continues in:
Love's Plea by Betty McLain

To read the first chapter for free, please head to:
https://www.nextchapter.pub/books/loves-plea

ABOUT THE AUTHOR

With five children, ten grandchildren and six great-grandchildren, I have a very busy life, but reading and writing have always been a very large and enjoyable part of my life. I have been writing since I was very young. I kept notebooks with my stories in them private. I didn't share them with anyone. They were all handwritten because I was unable to type. We lived in the country, and I had to do most of my writing at night. My days were busy helping with my brothers and sister. I also helped Mom with the garden and canning food for our family. Even though I was tired, I still managed to get my thoughts down on paper at night.

When I married and began raising my family, I continued writing my stories while helping my children through school and into their own lives and families. My sister was the only one to read my stories. She was very encouraging. When my youngest daughter started college, I decided to go to college myself. I had taken my GED at an earlier date and only had to take a class to pass my college entrance tests. I passed with flying colors and even managed to get a partial scholarship. I took computer classes to learn typing. The English and literature classes helped me to polish my stories.

I found public speaking was not for me. I was much more comfortable with the written word, but researching and writing the speeches was helpful. I could use information to build a story. I still managed to put my own spin on the essays.

I finished college with an associate degree and a 3.4 GPA. I had several awards, including President's List, Dean's List, and Faculty

List. The school experience helped me gain more confidence in my writing. I want to thank my English teacher in college for giving me more confidence in my writing by telling me that I had a good imagination. She said I told an interesting story. My daughter, who is a very good writer and has books of her own published, convinced me to have some of my stories published. She used her experience self-publishing to publish my stories them for me. The first time I held one of my books in my hands and looked at my name on it as author, I was so proud. They were very well received. This was encouragement enough to convince me to continue writing and publishing. I have been building my library of books written by Betty McLain since then. I also wrote and illustrated several children's books.

Being able to type my stories opened up a whole new world for me. Having access to a computer helped me to look up anything I needed to know and expanded my ability to keep writing my books. Joining Facebook and making friends all over the world expanded my outlook considerably. I was able to understand many different lifestyles and incorporate them in my ideas.

I have heard the saying, "Watch out what you say, and don't make the writer mad, you may end up in a book being eliminated." It is true. All of life is there to stimulate your imagination. It is fun to sit and think about how a thought can be changed to develop a story and to watch the story develop and come alive in your mind. When I get started, the stories almost write themselves; I just have to get all of it down as I think it before it is gone.

I love knowing the stories I have written are being read and enjoyed by others. It is awe-inspiring to look at the books and think, "I wrote that."

I look forward to many more years of putting my stories out there and hope the people reading my books are looking forward to reading them as much.

Lightning Source UK Ltd.
Milton Keynes UK
UKHW012001270720
367273UK00005B/313